WE OF THE BETWEEN

MARTII MACLEAN

KOOKY CAT BOOKS

Published by Kooky Cat Books 2017

Copyright © 2017 Martii Maclean

Book cover design and formatting services by BookCoverCafe.com

www.martiimaclean.com

ISBN:
978-0-9945408-4-3 (pbk)
978-0-9945408-5-0 (e-bk)

For Trevor *and* Minerva, *on watch in the lookout tower during my creative storms. Always at the ready with the life buoy when the waters get rough.*

New Canberra

High + Dry
New Sydney

S3

S4

S5

S1

S2

The Above

IN 1974, the Right Honourable Gough Whitlam, Prime Minister of Australia, signed the first federal initiative for environmental protection: to stop the Great Barrier Reef being exploited. He had the foresight to see the need to protect and prevent irreversible damage to the most precious asset humans had charge of — the seas and the earth.

Some humans had foresight but
many more chose not to see.

The Below

MANY LONG EONS AGO before humans wrote histories and before thoughts were words, the sea was home. Then the Abrax chose to walk on land, to give up their sleek twin tails and their mind songs and evolve, turning their backs on the sea.

But Mother Ocean cannot be ignored.
She is the beating heart that keeps the world alive.

THE ABOVE

F ish have a lot to say to each other. Trin would never have guessed this until the day the fish started talking to *her*. They had not always talked to her; it had started as a quiet whispering not so long ago and recently it had grown louder. She couldn't hear them all the time, just when she was in the water. It had been two days since she had last heard them talking, but she knew that would change as soon as she dipped her toe into the water.

She stood with her back pressed against the cliff wall in the narrow strip of shadow where it was cool. The neoprene wetskin she wore squeezed her, as if she was a foot wedged into a small shoe.

Stepping out into the sun, she could feel the warming dampness of sweat start to squelch inside the tight suit. She walked across the smooth rock, taking care not to step on the sharp ribbons of serration that pushed up where the rock had folded over on itself through the eons.

The sea was her place. She had swum before she could walk, and she felt more at ease in the water than on the rocky shore that was her home. Now the sea was speaking to her and it had become disquieting, but she still hungered to be in the water.

She dawdled towards the water's edge, sat down, took a deep breath, hesitating a little longer before she put her feet into the cool water. As soon as her skin made contact with the sea, the fish-talk started.

Strange sensations began flooding into her mind: a frittering, musical jangle that came from the fish signalling to each other as they dived and turned together. She knew what the fish signals meant, but what she didn't understand was *why* she knew what they meant. The signals were mostly emotions: curiosity, hunger, joy at new food, fear, all smashing together and pushing into her mind. It reminded her of the static she got sometimes from a bad download signal on the terminals when a storm was coming. She sat listening to the water bubbling and fizzing with messages being sent between the darting fish.

'I think I see ripples,' she called out to the rest of the fisher team, who were hauling the net across the rock ledge. 'It might be a school of fish.'

She had lied. She hadn't seen the fish, she had felt them, but she wasn't about to tell the team that. Sharly was the only one who knew anything about these weird fishy sensations, whatever they were.

'Yeah, I can see them swarming out at the end of the Funnel,' called Mal.

Trin was relieved Mal had called the sighting. Schools of fish had become increasingly rare since the warming, and Trin had been spotting nearly every catch lately. The team were starting to stir her about it.

Trying to ignore the fish signals, she slid into the water. The coolness instantly soothed her. The swell gently rocked her, buffeting and lifting her with a gentle nudge. She felt surrounded, cradled, and she let herself be rocked by the heartbeat rhythm of the ocean. The water lapped around her neck and face in salty tickles.

She lay back, allowing herself a moment, stretching out as though the ocean was a bed. Her body relaxed, lifting and falling with each swell. Her outstretched hand nudged the net, and she grabbed the nearest handhold as the rest of the team jumped into the water around her. It was time to catch fish.

She had been experimenting during the last few fishing trips, testing to see if the fish could hear her. She chose to experiment like this rather than freak out, afraid there might be something seriously wrong with her brain. After a few trials, she had come to accept the weird realisation that the fish were responding to her signals.

Here, fishy-fishy, come to the net.

The school suddenly turned around and headed towards the outstretched circle of net.

'Get ready,' called Mal.

'Always ready,' said Sharly.

The team worked well together. They angled the net, holding position, treading water, as the net filled. Then it bulged and began to shudder as the fish pushed and fought to find a way out of the trap.

Trin felt the fishes' distress, followed by her own guilt at trapping them and making them frightened and confused. She tried to push the guilt out of her mind. They needed the fish for food and breeding stock.

Fish were rare since the warming, so they respected catch limits to avoid overfishing. Conservation and replenishing the sea was what all the work at Whitlam Station was about, but knowing that didn't help Trin now. This strange new empathy she felt with the fish was frightening, and it was turning catching fish into something much harder than she thought it ever could be.

The fish were now frantic with fear. Trin could *feel— hear* the piscine equivalent of panicked screams. Jitters, odours and something she was sure were some sort of sonic distress calls flooded her mind as the nets closed around the catch. She was feeling the panic with the fish. Shaking her head, she tried to fling the signals out of her mind.

Burley! What is going on in my head?

Now she felt a new signal. From somewhere further out, in deeper water, shuddering feelings of *hunger— anger* burst into Trin's mind and flooded through her body like a hot wave. She sucked in a breath and choked on a mouthful of water.

Slam!

The blast of hunger and frustration hit her mind again, then a second angry surge. Trin squeezed her eyes closed as the pain of the signals tore through her head. The angry blast eased, becoming a chanting *thrum* that pulsed in the water around her and rippled through her body, forcing her heart to change its rhythm. She was held between these surging growls of hunger and anger, and the flitting panic from the fish fighting to be free of the nets.

The struggle between the opposing sensations held Trin frozen. She dropped down under the water. The trapped fish felt the thrumming threat coming closer and signalled to each other.

Danger—scatter.

Trin bobbed stiffly in the water as the anger and panic vibrated all around her.

'Trin! What are you doing?' called Mal.

Trin's fist was clenched tightly on the net, and she was being pulled along as the fisher team moved through the remaining school. 'Sorry,' she said, trying to bring her awareness back above the water. 'I thought I noticed something.'

'You okay, Trin?' called Sharly.

Hunger—food—close.

Trin could *hear* what the approaching creatures could hear: water rushing, like the pounding flow of a waterfall. She could smell what they could smell. The hungry animals could *smell* the panic coming from the netted fish. The smell sensation grew stronger, and so did the raw anticipation she felt coming from them.

She clenched her teeth. She knew. *Sharks!*

'Trin!'

She twisted around in the water to face the direction the signal was coming from, wanting to see, to confirm that it was sharks, wishing she was wrong. Her mind struggled against the jangling confusion coming from the nets and the surging fury pulsing out from the sharks. She kicked hard to lift herself higher up in the water, above the churning waves.

'I think I saw sharks,' she called out to the rest of the fishers. 'We should get us and the nets out now.'

'Are you sure, Trin?' Mal called back. 'The nets haven't been this full for ages.'

'And there's heaps more to catch, this school is massive,' added Raz.

'I'm sure,' said Trin. She twisted and looked out to sea again. She could feel the sharks closing in. 'Move!'

The team towed the bulging net towards the rock shelf. One by one, they scrambled awkwardly onto the rocks, each person keeping one hand straining on the net, which was growing heavier as it was drawn out of the water. Mal and Raz were already starting to pick the breeding stock out of the catch, placing them quickly into buckets of seawater to avoid shock.

Trin was out of the water now, and her ears rang with echoes of the signals. She let out a long sigh as she pulled up the net, watching the remains of the school escape, jittering through the water as they swarmed away from the rocks. She was thankful not to be feeling their panic anymore.

The fish were writhing in the net. She shuddered and gave a silent and sincere tribute: *Great thanks to the sea and her creatures for this sacrifice.*

'The nets could've been fuller,' moaned Tennan, 'but allegedly there are sharks. Where are they, Trin?'

'Oh, cut back, Tennan, and help haul in the catch,' snapped Sharly. 'At least we have a catch today after days of empty nets—thanks to Trin's spotting.'

Trin cringed. Sharly looked towards her and mouthed, *Sorry.*

'Yeah, thanks, Trin,' Tennan said. 'You're so amazing, why don't you help Sharly pull up our end of the net?' He let go of the net and stalked off.

Sharly braced against the extra load, but overbalanced and tumbled back into the water.

'It's cool, we've got it,' called Raz, as he and Mal grabbed the net before it and the remaining catch slipped back into the water.

7

'Not cool,' said Trin. 'Get out of the water, Sharls.'
Without hesitation, she jumped back in.

Trin's head filled instantly with the sharks' frenzy.
The scattering fish were leaving thick ribbons of panic
in the water, and the sharks were snapping blindly at the
scent trails. Trin held her position between Sharly and
the angry lamniformes.

This is my fault, she thought. *If it really was me who lured
the fish into nets, then the sharks are here because of me.*

With the fishes' panic and sharks' malignance
swirling around her, a new signal surged into her mind, a
different signal, a wave of concern, a hot, anxious disquiet
about her and Sharly. Then it vanished and was replaced
by a compulsion that filled Trin's mind to bursting.

Decoy!

She felt compelled to divert the sharks to give Sharly
time to get out of the water. But how?

'Sharls, *out*!' Trin shoved Sharly towards the rocks,
then duck-dived under the water and swam away from
her friend.

The feeling was there again, and a signal: *schooling
fish*. Trin found she was imagining herself surrounded by
a roiling cloud of shimmering fish. And as she did, she
sensed the sharks' attention turning away from Sharly
and towards her, their frenzy growing. *Good one, Trin,
you've just made yourself the target of a feeding frenzy.*

The sharks closed in.

Hunger.

Trin was in the middle of her own illusion because of a strangely irresistible impulse.

Schooling fish.

Trin reimagined the school. The sharks fanned out, surrounding her. They were attempting to flank the imaginary school of fish.

'Trin, get *out*!' screamed Sharly, struggling to get free of Mal, who was holding her arm.

Trim felt the displaced water pressing against her as the sharks sped past.

Anger.

They were shaking their broad heads from side to side in frustration. She could feel the swirling current as they turned to take another run at Trin's fake school.

Hunger.

Their jaws snapped aimlessly in the hope of contacting with food. As they sped in again, Trin squeezed her eyes closed. She felt a heavy thud on one side of her body and waited for the pain, the tearing, the swirls of blood. She could hear Sharly screaming and the others yelling from the rocks.

There was no blood. She had copped a thump in the ribs from a shark as it had hammered through the imaginary school she had conjured, but nothing worse. The school! Trin had stopped making her illusion. She held her breath and waited for the next attack. Nothing. The sharks had suddenly turned away.

Trin could sense the remainder of the school that had escaped the nets, swarming and circling around the end of the Funnel. It seemed strange that they hadn't scattered when they sensed the sharks. Why would the fish reform the school then stay near danger?

The thrumming signal of *malevolence* from the sharks suddenly subsided and was replaced by another: *satisfaction*. They had caught their prey and were feasting.

Then the other signal returned, for a brief moment: *relief*. *Relief?* Then it was gone.

Sharly dived back into the water and swam towards Trin. They were as close as any friends could be, but the *relief* signal had not come from Sharly. Trin's head swum with the jumble of fading sensations: fish, sharks and that strange signal of *relief*.

'Trin,' said Sharly, wrapping her arm around Trin's chest, ready to rescue her. Trin didn't need rescuing, but her mind felt bruised and battered so she was glad not to be alone. She would let Sharly help her back to the water's edge.

But within three strokes, Sharly stopped. Trin heard a deep sob rise in her friend's throat. Sharly broke from the rescue grip and turned to face her.

'You saved me, Trin,' Sharly choked out. 'Thank you.'

'Of course I did, we're buddies.'

'The sharks could've killed you.'

Trin hugged Sharly. 'But they didn't. They followed the fish.'

'Did you do that? Like the other fish thing?'

10

'Maybe.' Trin shook her aching head. 'I don't know.'

Sharly was crying. 'Thank you,' she said again, and went to put Trin back in a rescue hold.

'Hey, you'll end up suffering noodle arms,' Trin said, trying to make her friend smile. 'I can rescue myself now.' She gave Sharly another quick hug and they turned toward the shore.

As she swam, Trin looked along the rock ledge and across the cliff face, which was studded with caves. Her gaze stopped on her father, who was rappelling down the escarpment. He reached the bottom and unhooked his harness from one of the ropes that everyone called snakes—a match for the ladders they used to climb up the cliffs.

Meg, the station coordinator, came out of the main lab to meet him, and they both jogged towards the fishers.

As the girls clambered up out of the water, Trin waved. 'Hi, Dad, hi, Meg.'

Neither Meg nor Trin's father waved back. Their faces were like twin storm clouds.

THE BELOW

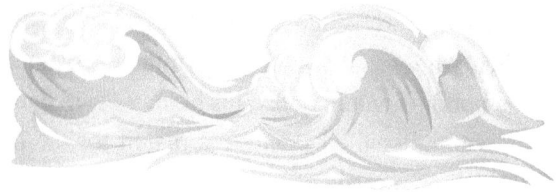

All was quiet when Rilla woke. Blinking away her drowsiness, she uncoiled her tails and slowly floated up from the rocky dish that was her nest. She twisted and turned, stretching and feeling the ribbons of current, warm-cool, as they flowed across her skin. Warm-cool, as they oscillated around inside the great cavern, where their constant movements caused the sea plants to sway like a dance. Warm-cool as the currents refreshed the water and kept it clean and clear.

The day was just beginning. The light from above had barely found its way through the narrow shafts in the domed rock above to lighten the darkness of the enormous vaulted city cavern of Lemuria.

Rilla stretched herself again and gazed across the lower slopes surrounding the city. The city at night was lit by the gentle glow of the luminous blue dots that were the countless other sleeping Abrax, who were curled in the nests that were scattered around the dished floor of the great cave.

Spiralling, she drifted further from her nest. With each turn, she viewed the city anew. Through the blue-on-blue twilight, she could see meeting places and trading points, and the abundant gardens of coral surrounding the glowing tower of the Hall of Colours, by far the most imposing structure in Lemuria, its grandness matching its importance to the Abrax. For this was the place where all Abrax gathered for ceremonies and to seek counsel with Thal and Ula, Rilla's parents, the elected rulers of the city.

A warm current lifted her. She twisted and tumbled as she rose, taking in the tranquil scene. High in the darker reaches of the domed cavern, she saw shafts of teal light leaking in through several round entrances. The sun was rising in the world of the Above.

Rilla loved waking early, when she could be truly alone in the peace of her own thoughts without the neumes from the minds of the other Abrax intruding. She could shield herself from these exchanges of the mind. All Abrax could ignore the neumes of others with little effort, but Rilla enjoyed the true peace of these moments before the deep blues faded into day. At this time, she could be truly alone with her private thoughts. In the early morning while everyone still slept, she could stare up through the lightening water, imagining the Above, which lay beyond the surface. She could wonder without needing to guard her thoughts from any minds that might judge her.

Rilla stopped her imagining before anyone else woke and discovered her neumes. She spiralled down and stared dreamily at the bioluminescent shapes of her sleeping sisters, Lana and Neeva. They looked so beautiful, glowing warm orange and crimson against the blue-green of the rock nest they shared.

Rilla didn't have her colours yet, but she knew it would be soon. She had been so restless lately and her skin itched terribly. Her moult would happen, and then she would shed the dull brown skin of a youngling and enter her choosing time.

Stretching again, she pushed away the last of the drowsiness and realised that something felt different today. She tried to focus on what she was feeling. No, what she *wasn't* feeling. It was an absence.

She was no longer feeling itchy.

She held out her arms and looked at them, and then flicked out both her tails. Her skin was smooth and shining, with a pearl rainbow of colours glistening across its surface. Yesterday there had only been the silty brown skin of a youngling, itching and peeling. The remains of her shed skin lay in curls in the nest, beside her sleeping sisters.

The moult had happened while she slept. She was a changeling, finally.

She stared back up at the brightening shafts of light and fizzed with excitement. Now that she was a mature Abrax, she could go to the surface without breaking the rules.

Rilla had argued often that she was surely ready to go to the surface, to the bright Above, but she knew she would never get permission from her father until she had moulted and entered her choosing time. That's why she had broken the rule and taken advantage of rare opportunities to creep away and drift up to take a look at the Above, even though she knew it was forbidden to go alone and absolutely forbidden for younglings.

While she had been in the Above, blinking in the glistening brightness, she had held her gills closed and raised her head as far as she dared above the water. She had watched the steady world of rock and soil, and imagined what it would be like to walk there on the land. What it would be like to *walk*—to have legs instead of tails.

At last she was grown. Now she could surface and take air, as every changeling had a right to do in preparation for the choosing ceremony. It was the right of every Abrax to choose to live as an adult in Lemuria, or change and ascend to the Above.

Rilla had never known of anyone who had ascended, and neither had her sisters, but the choice to remain in the Below as an Abrax, or change and ascend to live in the Above, was an important right that marked the transition into the adult community of the city.

All young Abrax eagerly awaited the tradition of the choosing, but having that right to ascend was especially tantalising for Rilla. She had seen the Above from a distance, and now she imagined walking and exploring that solid, strange place, meeting the walkers who lived there, and finding out about them and their life in the Above. She burned with curiosity.

She looked at her new, luminescent skin and smiled. She could see the ripples of pearly colour that flowed across her skin, showing the absolute joy she was feeling at entering her choosing time. *Finally!*

Rilla swirled around in colourful, bubbling circles, spiralling up away from her nest, until she floated high up in the city dome. *Today it's gone*, she neumed, feeling her head pounding with the intensity of the joyous message. *Today I am grown.*

Congratulations, Rilla, came a soothing message from her eldest sister Lana, who was stretching as she floated up from the nest towards her. *You'll have the whole of Lemuria awake soon.*

You surely will, neumed Neeva in agreement, *but on a day like today it's all about you, baby sister. Today you are grown.* Neeva circled up and wrapped her tails affectionately around Rilla's, tangling her in a spiralling, knotted hug.

Today I can take air, neumed Rilla excitedly. *And sing instead of ping.*

Don't let father know you think we 'ping', warned Neeva. *Our neumes are nothing like pings. Dolphins ping, and we can barely make sense of it.*

I can't wait to go up and breathe the air and sing. Rilla spun around excitedly, causing another frenzied vortex of bubbles.

Her sisters gently took an arm each, putting an end to her spinning celebration.

Remember, it's forbidden to go to the surface alone, Lana reminded her. *You need to be vigilant against those who live in the Above. And first breath isn't something you should do alone. The pain and the burning ... you know you never have to do it; you never have to take that breath. We were given the right to choose, and we celebrate to show we're worthy and wise before we decide on a life in the Above or the Below. But why would you want to be ... up there?* Lana pulled a face, her shiny skin momentarily fading to grey-brown, showing her distaste.

Some Abrax chose the Above, didn't they? Rilla neumed. *Chose to walk in the Above and never returned?*

That was millennia ago, Rilla, Neeva replied, *and you'll see how the Above changed them. I'll show you. They're very different from us now.*

They're dull and brown now and they can no longer return to the sea, added Lana. *Their gills shrivelled from always breathing air, and now they're trapped up there, in their foul, poisoned world. Surrounded by all the filth the walkers have created.*

Neeva squeezed Rilla's hand. *You've had your lessons, so you know that in the Above they've sullied and ruined much of the world, and now the sea is sick and angry because of the poison. Mother Ocean is rising up, flooding over the land, trying to wash away the hurt from the walker world so the healing can begin.*

Mother Ocean will need to fight hard, neumed Lana. *Because of the heat from all the damage the walkers have done, the great ice is melting, and the melted water has diluted the salty seas. The diluted water is making Mother and her creatures sick. The currents are colder and fiercer, and now things are dying because of the damage done by those filthy, selfish walkers.*

Maybe these changes are a sign that we should change, too. Rilla glowed with ripples of pale blue-green, showing her concern for the state of Mother Ocean. *Maybe if we could meet with the walkers we could share our knowledge with them, help them with the healing and make things better for the Below and the Above.*

Don't let anyone know you have ideas like that, Rilla, or you'll be sent to the Deeps for sure, warned Lana.

The Deeps are a myth, snapped Rilla, *a tale to frighten younglings into being obedient.*

Lana turned and grabbed Rilla's shoulders. *The Deeps are real, little sister*, she cautioned harshly. *The guards know things and they share little secrets with me. Sometimes I creep into their minds without their knowing.* Lana's skin glowed golden; she was proud of her sneaky dealings. *The guards had neumed about taking troublesome Abrax to the Deeps to be retrained by elders or some such. I haven't found out all the details yet, but it's true. The guards seemed frightened of the Deeps and when they saw me, they guarded their thoughts. They have other secrets; I know it.*

Rilla shook herself free from Lana's grip. *I don't believe you. Father thinks he can control all the souls of the Abrax with fear. Just because he rules Lemuria it doesn't mean he can tell us how to live our lives.* Rilla's skin flashed a glowing deep red of angry frustration. She hated the idea of being forced to ignore that the Above and Below were connected just to please her father. *Maybe Father has influence over the Abrax during their choosing. We've never personally known a soul to choose to ascend.*

Perhaps no one has chosen to ascend since we were born. Why would they? Lana's neume pushed hard into Rilla's mind. *Father respects the traditions.*

Of course he does. Neeva smoothed a tail over Lana and radiated a calm blue. *We, all Abrax, get to choose between living here in the Below or ascending to live in the Above. Maybe it's been a long time since someone has chosen to ascend.*

Neeva coiled her tails around Rilla's and smiled. *This is your shedding day, Rilla. We should concentrate on enjoying the beginning of your celebrations.*

You have three moons to decide about your choosing, neumed Lana, *though I can't see why anyone would want a life in the Above.*

Let's go and share the great tidings with Mother and Father. Neeva disentangled her tails from Rilla's and nudged her down towards the Hall of Colours, where their parents would be waking.

And don't be in a hurry to go above, warned Lana, as she drifted on the other side of Rilla. *You know you can't go alone or Father will be rancorous.*

Okay, I'll wait, Rilla lied, as they descended together.

She wanted to be alone when she sang. Her feelings of being drawn to the Above were strange and strong, and she felt compelled to explore and consider them in private. She didn't want her first proper experiences of the Above to be tainted by neumes of caution and corrupted myths, designed to force her to choose in favour of the Below. Rilla believed that if the walkers could perceive the world from the sea, the way the Abrax did, and if they could share the Abrax knowledge, they would understand what needed to be done to heal both their worlds.

So you'll come with me when I sing? She glowed a passive blue, hoping to convince her sisters that she would wait and not visit the Above alone.

No, Lana neumed fiercely, *I've made my choice and I never want to see the Above again.*

I'll go with you, neumed Neeva, tangling her tails with Rilla's as they neared the Hall of Colours.

Rilla knew that once inside the hall, they would declare the day of her moulting to their parents and the other Abrax gathered there, and the beginning of the three-moon season of her choosing time would be celebrated with a feast in her honour.

THE ABOVE

Fish guts flew up into the air, followed by a frenzy of squawking as the gulls swooped and dived, performing amazing aerial stunts to fill their beaks with the rare and apparently delicious guts. The hungry, hopeful gulls circled in the air above the fishers as they scaled and cleaned their catch.

'The guts are for the gardens,' said Meg.

'Yeah,' said Tennan. 'But the gulls put on a great show to get a mouthful of this burley. Watch.' He waved a thin sausage of intestine in the air. 'Here, pathetic little scavengers, come and get your gross guts.' He flung the wet garland into the air and the gulls became feathered sharks, snapping and snarling at each other to get to the food.

'Frube,' mumbled Mal. 'He's got burley for brains.'

'Enough, Tennan,' scolded Meg. 'We need that offal for fertiliser up at the gardens. The soil up there can barely grow a teatree without it, and we need the vegetables. It's too far and too costly to keep going to High and Dry to pick up vegies we could grow ourselves with a little effort.'

'There's nothing for the gulls to catch out there.' Sharly pointed across the water. 'They're struggling as much as we are to get food from the sea.'

'True. When the salinity drops so do the fish numbers,' agreed Meg quietly. 'Okay. Just one more piece.'

Trin had moved as slowly as she could while she was getting changed out of her wetskin, and now she kept her head down and concentrated on pulling a long, stretching line of intestines out of the slit she had just made in the silver belly of a fish. She knew her dad was watching her, waiting to fill her ears with his latest lecture about taking risks, but while everyone was here, all he could do was glare at her. Maybe if she kept her head down long enough he would give up and return to his work in the lab.

She passed the gutted bream to Mal, who was waiting, tapping his knife on the gutting stand. He took the fish and flashed her a tiny smile. He knew the way she handled her father—by avoiding confrontation.

She reached for another fish, deciding to slow down even more. Her dad was starting to look a little red-faced. She didn't think he would wait much longer.

'Trin …' her father began, then looked around and stalled.

I knew he'd get restless, Trin thought. Any second now …

'Can you bring a pan-sized one to the lab for me when you're done?' he said. Then he added quietly, 'I want to talk to you.'

'Totally, Dad, see you as soon as I'm done,' she said, without looking up.

Trin knew that sometimes when her dad was feeling sentimental he liked to go to the headland and cook a fish in a pan over a fire, like he used to do with her mum. But when he was feeling sentimental it usually meant he was also feeling over-protective, and that meant his lecture would probably be massive. She slowed down some more, pretending she'd tangled her fingers in the fish's digestive tract.

'Come on, Trin, why so slow?' teased Mal.

'Cut back, Mal,' she snapped.

'Because maybe she doesn't want to talk with her dad,' said Meg, picking up the fat bream. 'Go and give this to him, Trin, and get the lecture over with.'

'Meg, you know what he's like about me being in the water so much,' said Trin.

'And you know why that is.' Meg nudged her shoulder affectionately. 'It's just you and him now, so he worries about losing you, too. Give him a break. Take the fish and go get your lecture over and done with.'

Trin stuck her fingers into the bream's gills and let it swing limply by her side as she dawdled along the rock ledge. Her dad's lab was at the far end of the cliff, and she hoped that if she walked slowly enough he would be caught up in his work again by the time she got there.

She walked into the coolness of the lab cave, holding the fish in front of her like a peace offering. She hoped he was too engrossed in his work to be cross with her. 'I know you're busy with work, Dad,' she said, 'so I won't hold you up. Here, Meg chose a fat one for you.' Putting the fish down in the pan that always sat on the bench nearest the door, she turned to make her escape.

'I'll thank her later,' said her dad. 'Now what the hell were you doing out there?'

Trin stopped, sighed, and turned back around to face her father. 'Just doing what we always do, Dad. Trying to contribute to the project by helping to collect viable breeding stock and keep everyone at Whitlam Station fed,' she said, sounding like a training vid-file.

'I appreciate the team spirit, but you saw the sharks. You never miss seeing anything. All the kids talk about how "tuned in" you are. I watched you as I was coming down the snake. You stayed out there, the last in with the net. Then you jumped back in.'

'But Sharly needed me.'

'Damn, Trin, I saw the sharks swim right past you.' His voice faltered.

25

She pressed her lips together; feeling guilty relief that neither her dad nor Meg had seen how close the sharks had come to her. She folded her arms self-consciously in front of her tender ribs.

'They were only after the school, Dad,' she said, trying to console him. 'The sharks were always going to turn and follow the rest of the school. I was fine. I've been spending so much time in the water I'm getting a real sense of how the fish and other animals behave.'

'You spend too much time in the water, just like your mother did,' he snapped.

'But, Dad, nothing ever attacked her in the water either.'

Her dad seemed to fold in on himself for a moment. Trin was instantly sorry she had used her mum as a way to try and win the argument. Yes, her mum had always been safe in the water, but she had died anyway, and Dad hadn't been able to help her.

Meg had told Trin a little about the day her mother died. Her father had found her lying at the high-tide line. Trin wondered why, if her mum knew she was that sick, she had chosen to be there, at the end, lying alone at the edge of the sea rather than in the arms of the man who loved her.

'Sorry, Dad.'

'No, it's true, she was always safe in the water.' He straightened up and became Dad again. 'But, Little Fish,' he said, using her nickname, 'the sea is so unpredictable. Everything's changed since the warming and the seas' rising.

We're still discovering things we didn't expect. I don't want you to be a victim to something we don't know about yet.'

'I'm sorry, Dad, I didn't mean to scare you. I just love being out there.'

'I know you do, Fish, just like your mum did.'

'Dad, will you tell me more about what Mum was like? Meg told me she used to help in the fish-catching teams, too. That she had a knack of knowing where to cast the nets. I was just wondering if she ever said how she did it. How she knew where the fish would be.'

'What, you think you've inherited some sort of fish radar, or something?' He laughed gently and his face softened. 'I don't think so, Trin, but you're obsessed with the sea just like she was. And wilful.' He sighed deeply and turned back to his workbench.

'But can we talk about her some more, Dad? Maybe while you cook the fish?'

He stared at the fish and his eyes glossed with tears. He blinked them away and turned to face her again. 'It's too hard for me, Little Fish, I'm sorry.' He hugged her tight.

'No sweat, Dad.'

'Talk to Meg, she knew your mum as long as I did. She might be able to tell you what you want to know.' He turned his glassy eyes back to his work.

Trin left the lab and walked along the rock shelf. The day was getting cooler in the deepening shadows of the cliff, but the rock felt warm under her feet as she walked.

Stopping at the bottom rung of the first of the ladders that zigzagged up the cliff face to the cave she shared with Sharly, she watched the rest of the team laughing at the aerial circus of squabbling gulls. She looked out across the calm sea, took a shuddering breath and decided to head up to her cave.

THE BELOW

The Abrax were given three moons to celebrate being changelings and ponder on their decision: stay in the Below, or ascend to become a walker and live in the Above. Before the choosing day, every changeling was to be escorted to the surface to observe the Above in preparation for the tradition of taking air and making their song as a declaration of their choice.

The choosing process was conducted with great solemnity and could not be rushed. In the months leading up to the ceremony, each changeling was expected to keep their neumes private, and they could ask to visit the Above as many times as they thought they needed to.

Rilla was thrilled that no one was expecting to share her thoughts, which meant she would not accidentally share that she had secretly visited the Above alone many times to observe the walkers. With each visit, she had moved a little closer to the shore. She had held her breath as she watched and listened. Her choosing time had started long ago.

She had made up her mind. Today would be her song day.

The song would tell both worlds, the Above and the Below, about her choice. She knew what her choice would be, and because of this she didn't want a witness to her song. How would her family react when she neumed that she had chosen to take the catalyst and ascend? She decided that these concerns could wait; she had almost two moons remaining before being expected to choose.

Once outside the domed expanse of the cavern that protected and concealed Lemuria, Rilla swam hard, heading upwards. The water faded from darkest indigo through cobalt, azure, sapphire and lightest turquoise as she drew closer to the surface. At last, a pale blue brightness surrounded her and she held herself, floating face up, just below the swelling surface of the sea. The sun danced on the water, refracting with dazzling unpredictability. Knives of light pierced down through the warm blue all around her.

Rilla remained there, looking up at the sky through the rippling water. She wondered how much it would hurt when she let the air from the Above into her lungs for the first time. Would it hurt again as she pushed the air out to make her song? Everyone had neumed that the air would feel hot, like lava from the vents in the Deeps. That she would burn, but not be charred.

Rilla stopped the sculling that was holding her under the water and let her body bob up to the surface. She felt the familiar coolness of the wind on her wet skin. How could this cool air possibly burn her? Everything about her surroundings was astonishing, and although everything seemed strange and frightening at first, nothing in the Above had ever done her any harm.

During her first visits, she had dared to stay only moments. She had only raised her head above the water, and gazed around at the blazing blue sky and the dots of distant colour that were the world of the Above. But with each visit she had ventured further, eventually swimming close to the shore and finding walkers there. She had watched, fascinated by their movements and the sounds they made as their air-words carried across the waves.

Once she had even felt a neume coming from the shore, from the mind of a walker. She didn't know how that could be. Walkers had left the oceans so long ago, and they didn't need to neume in the Above. She burned with curiosity to find out why this should be and to find out everything else she could about the walkers. She had made her decision. Now she needed to be brave enough to take a breath and sing out her choice.

Rilla opened her lips a fraction, just enough to let the air trickle into her mouth. It felt cool, like the wind when it danced on her wet skin. She opened her mouth wider and the coolness travelled down her throat and filled her chest, but there was no burning. She closed her mouth and a few tiny bubbles fizzed out from the gill-folds that ran in a narrow, rippling line from each side of her neck towards her shoulders. She parted her lips and let the air escape. It had been warmed while it was inside her body, but it didn't burn at all.

The burning is a myth, she neumed. *Maybe I'm not doing this correctly.*

Bracing herself for pain, she drew in a big lungful of air, and felt a twinge and some bubbling down low in her chest. Then there was a gurgling spasm, her throat constricted and her chest convulsed, pushing the air back out. Water rushed out with the air and Rilla made a breathy, barking sound like the seals did when they lay on the shore. Water sprayed from her mouth and leaked from her nose. Bubbles of air pushed through her gill-folds, causing a fizzy, tickling sensation. All these happenings were startling, but still there was no burning.

The fizzing of the air moving in her throat and through her gills felt delightful. She had stopped barking now and started making a strange huffing sound in her throat.

This strange huffing felt pleasant, it seemed to go with her feelings of astonishment and relief that there was no burning, and her amusement about the strange way air moved around her body.

She wondered if the walkers made this huffing noise and what it might signal. She added this to the endless questions she had about the Above.

Reflecting on all her experiences since coming to the Above, Rilla steadied her thoughts. She took a deep, purposeful breath and began her song. Rilla's song was very different from the neume-songs the Abrax felt and sent to each other in waves of thought. It was a blend of the sounds she had heard with her ears on her many visits to the Above. She blended birdsong with the mysterious, distant melodies she had heard blown on the breeze from the walkers on the shore.

She was glad she had chosen to be on her own. Neeva would have been witness to her song, and if her sister had heard this unknown walker tune she would have realised it was something from the Above, and then Rilla's secret visits would have been discovered. If Neeva had been a witness, she would have carried the cruel burden of Rilla's deception.

It would have made no difference anyway, Rilla decided. Her song was a declaration of her choosing, a celebration of her decision to ascend. Rilla now had two moons in which to neume on how to tell her family about her choice.

Rilla's song rose in her throat, powered by the absolute delight she was feeling at this moment. Her song swelled up and down like the ocean, and she sent it out far through the warm air. The birds answered her song and joined in her joyous celebration.

When her song ended, she lay floating on the undulating water with the sun warming her skin. The sunlight glowed pink through her closed eyelids. She played with the new pleasure of breathing, closing her lips and forcing fizzing bubbles through her gills. Then she smiled and her body made the huffing sound in response to the silliness of the sensation.

How could I not choose the Above?

Lying back, she let the undulating sea cradle her as she imagined the new life she would have in the Above.

Something seized one of her tales. She gasped and tried to twist away. Whatever it was, it was clenched firmly around both her tails. Rilla cried out in pain as she was tugged roughly and dragged below the water.

THE ABOVE

The ladders were steep, but Trin took the steps two at a time, mumbling word after frustrated word with each footfall.

'Why … can't … Dad … just … tell … me … something? At … least … he … gets … to … miss … Mum … but … I … can't … ever … get … to … know … her. He … won't … let … me.'

She was breathing hard when she reached the cave and flopped down inside the circular entrance. Staring out to sea, she tried to dispel her resentment. She let her focus soften until the sky and the sea melted into a glistening, blue haze.

Trin had been very young when her mother died. Her dad only ever shared tiny things about her, and they always seemed to be cautionary tales. Trin wished he would tell her more. At least being able to hold onto conjured memories would be better than the nothing she had right now.

She thought about the fish-talk again and wondered if some of the old stories about her mum might hold some clues. Maybe Dad or Meg would say something about her mother that matched up with what Trin had been experiencing. What if the things that were happening to her had come about since the warming and the rising seas? The reports from all the stations were full of plenty of evidence of mutation in the fish as they struggled to survive the changes, but maybe it affected humans, too.

'Well, there are some great options,' Trin whispered. 'I can be sick, I can be going nuts or I'm a mutant freak. Awesome.'

Trin stayed there, at the mouth of the cave she shared with Sharly, dangling her feet over the edge, staring out across the water. The sea's mood seemed to be changing to match hers. The sky had darkened and the water was becoming a grey-black stew of chopping, white-topped waves, jostling and shoving each other like they were picking a fight. The sea never did what it was predicted to do since the rising, but everyone at the station had learned to live with it. They did endless drills to learn about the safety gear and emergency procedures. Trin could remember doing them ever since she could walk.

At Whitlam Station, kids had nearly as many responsibilities as adults, or that's the way it felt when there was work to do. The good side of that was they also had privileges like other station team members.

Last year, Trin and Sharly had petitioned to move out of their family digs and share a cave. Trin's dad worked all the time, anyway, so he didn't have much reason to object. Station management had approved their application and the girls had moved to the topmost row of caves. Trin loved being up high. It gave her a massive view of the ocean, all the way to the horizon, up and down the coast. The climb up the ladders was an effort some days, but abseiling back down the snakes was always crankin'.

It's getting rowdy out there, Trin thought. A storm was coming. It was easy to predict the storms but harder to know how big the storm surge would be. Lately, though, Trin always knew. In a similar way to the signals coming from the fish, she could feel the sea's moods building inside her.

She shuddered. Today they would need the cave doors to be sealed against the hammering walls of water, even this high up the cliff.

Trin's attention was drawn away from the sea. She let her gaze sweep along the rock ledge that curved around to the end of the peninsula, then across the narrow channel they called the Blender, which was lined with sharp fangs of rock, and out to Lighthouse Island on the other side.

The island, which used to be part of the peninsula until it was cut off permanently by the rising water, was a large mound of rock on top of which stood an old crumbling lighthouse. The lighthouse had fascinated Trin since she was a child, but the rule about the island was for everyone at the station: no one was to cross the Blender, ever, for any reason. That passage of water was the most unpredictable part of this always-unpredictable environment, so no one ever broke that rule.

The older station personnel had distant memories of all the things that had changed since the rising, but Trin and the others on the fisher team hadn't known the coast to be any different from the way it was now. This landscape was normal for Trin and Sharly and the others, and it was a cool place to be if you were as familiar with the grumpy sea as they had become by having grown up at Whitlam Station. So they didn't break the blender rule, but they did sometimes slightly bend some of the others.

One day Mal had discovered old vid-files of his grandfather surfing at an actual beach with actual sand. He also found some bizarre old surf movies from maybe a hundred years ago, along with his granddad's journals.

They had laughed a lot, watching the video, and it had given them some great ideas, for which rule breaking would be necessary. But knowing the fear and the loss people felt when everything started flooding was wretched, and reading Mal's grandfather's journal was sad.

'… slept overnight in the carpark, huddled up in the back of the van like a litter of puppies. This beach is crankin'. Best breaks, least storm erosion, one of the last beaches left so I guess that makes it the favourite. I woke as the first glow of the day came over the curve of the ocean and tapped on my eyelids. I scrambled from the van and stood there just watching. At this time of day, you can see the earth turning, almost feel it moving under your feet. The others got up and we oozed ourselves into our worn-out wetsuits, grabbed our boards and headed down the track and across the cold sand and pushed out into the foaming surf.

The ocean is a creature. A big wet dragon, powerful, moody. You need to know those moods and respect them or she'll kill you. We paddled out towards the rising sun, working through the ridges of waves, like the spiny scales on the dragon's back. I've never smiled so much as when I was out there, behind the breaks, waiting for the next set. It was smooth as glass. The ocean rose and fell. You could feel the dragon breathing, calm as you like. We'd wait. Then the waves would come in pounding rows.

I would choose the wave and lay down on the board, wetsuit squeak-squeaking, as I paddled as though the devil was behind me. Then the dragon would lift me into her shiny tumbling claws and fling me towards the beach. I'd stand with my feet wide and dance with the dragon, wishing I had hands for feet. I'd ride the wave in and then paddle out and do it again and again and again. I never forgot to respect the dragon …'

'It must've been so scary when everything started flooding,' Mal had said quietly when he stopped reading. 'And how burley, when Granddad realised they would never surf again. It seems like massive fun.'

'We won't get to surf like your granddad did, but there's no point wasting the terminology. It's *crankin'*,' Trin had said, mimicking the words from the journal and the movies.

'Sick,' said Mal, and they had laughed until they snorted.

Those old movies had given them an ancient set of code words that only they knew, so they could keep discussion of their rule-breaking activities private. After seeing the old files they knew what was changed and gone forever. They couldn't miss the coastline they'd never known, but by using the old words they kept the beaches alive in a small way. And using them was ridiculous fun.

The memories lightened Trin's mood, and soon she was hum-mumbling, 'For every grain of sand that's on the beach ...'

'... I've got a kiss for you.' Meg appeared at the top of the ladder and Trin snapped out of her musical daydream. Meg climbed in, shrugged off her backpack and sat next to her on the ledge. 'You still remember that old song? Your mum used to sing it to you all the time.'

'I guess I do.' Trin shrugged.

'Did your dad give you a hard time?'

'Not really.' Trin shrugged again. 'I apologised for scaring him. You know what he's like. He's still so sad, and then he fills his head with work to push the sadness out. With all the sadness and the science, there's not much room for me, not for too long anyway.'

'Come on, Trin, he loves you. I watched how he was with you when you were little. Anyone who saw him then would have thought you were the first baby on the planet, not just the first one born at Whitlam. He never stopped talking about his "Little Fish".'

'But then Mum got sick ...'

'He loved her so much, Trin. He was sort of washed out to sea when she died, but he always made sure he spent time with you.'

'Well, he still seems lost at sea most days, and he treats me like I might dissolve if I do anything other than study.'

'He worries, Fish.'

Only her dad and Meg called her Fish. Meg tried to help out when she could, and Trin liked that.

'He worries about you. And when you're sick, he panics that you're getting sick like your mum did.'

'But whatever my sickness is, it isn't like what Mum had. She...' Trin stopped short of saying *I can't have what Mum had because I'm not dead*. 'I never get sick in summer, when I can swim more. Dad should unshackle, he's always stopping me from spending time in the water.'

'You do seem to be more afflicted in the colder weather, but people get sick in winter. That's not news to a doctor,' said Meg. 'At least winter's not as cold as it used to be.'

Trin stared out to sea.

Meg nudged her shoulder. 'Climate joke,' she said.

'I thought he'd be proud of me.' Trin kept her eyes fixed on the dark clouds churning in from the horizon. 'I study all those extra modules so I can get into marine bio one day and stay here at Whitlam and train with you guys. What about the catch? We've been catching so much more fish lately. Now we can send heaps of breeding stock out to High and Dry.'

'He is proud of you, Trin, but the sea is unpredictable and he worries. Let him do his Dad thing. Your mum used to spend hours in the water, too, and he was always obsessed by the thought that it was the sea that made her sick somehow.'

'Being in the water cranks.'

'Cranks?'

'Um, it feels good. I feel strong there. I swim fast and …' She stopped, wondering if she should tell Meg about sensing the fish and the sharks, and the weird other thing she thought she sensed today.

'So you feel great and strong. That's good to hear, now let me give you a bit of a check-up to back up your claims.' Meg smiled and started pulling equipment out of the backpack for the examination.

'Tell me a story about Mum,' Trin asked, as Meg poked at her and mumbled. 'Dad doesn't tell me anything when I ask him.'

'What do you want to know?'

'What was she good at?' Trin didn't know how to ask if her mother could talk to fish. 'Did she have special tasks? All Dad tells me is that she loved being in the sea, and that she was really committed to making things better by helping breed fish that could handle the drop in salinity levels. I want to know what she was like without the science.'

'Loving the sea is part of the job description for marine scientists,' Meg said, 'and yes, she did seem to have a stronger connection to the water than any of us. And she knew so much. I remember when she arrived. The station was just getting established. She'd come up from Mawson Station, doing a networking visit to compare procedures and data. I don't think your dad heard a thing she said about her work and her findings.

He just stared at her, captivated. They worked together every day after that. Your mum's knowledge of the coastline and currents and temperatures was faultless. She was a valuable asset to the station. One day she announced she'd applied to transfer to us permanently. No surprise there, considering the way your mum and dad looked at each other. Not long after that, we held their wedding and then there was you.'

'Taa-daa.' Trin took a little bow.

Meg smiled. 'I performed the wedding, you know.'

'And her funeral,' Trin whispered.

Meg crumpled a little. 'That's what station leaders do, Fish.'

Trin grabbed her hand. 'Well, thanks for performing their wedding, or maybe there wouldn't have been a Trin.' They both laughed. 'You said Mum had lots of skills,' Trin said, pushing. 'Was she as good a fisher as me?'

'She did have a bit of a knack for dropping a net in just the right place.'

'So do I pass your tests? I don't have what Mum had, do I?' She wasn't sure if she was saying that to convince Meg or herself.

'You do pass my tests, but you're looking awfully pale, Fish.' Meg ran her hand up Trin's usually tanned arm and then touched her cheek. 'Any paler and you'd glow,' she teased. 'You should get an early night.'

The sun was setting and the inside of the cave was now in deep shadow. Trin's skin was definitely paler than usual, lots paler. She ground her teeth together, scrambling for a response. 'I must've swum through a bloom out there during the fish harvest.'

Her heart was thumping. She knew it wasn't an algal bloom making her look pale. She had noticed it a few weeks ago, just after the *fish-talk* started. Each time she experienced the strange fish sensations, she looked pale and washed out. Things were changing and she didn't have explanations for any of them.

'I haven't had a shower yet. After visiting Dad it slipped my mind.' She rubbed at her arms.

'Are you sure? I really should do some more tests,' Meg said. The storm siren sounded. 'But that'll have to wait.' She quickly piled things back into her pack and shrugged it on. 'Get sealed in, quick.' She clicked her harness onto the *snake* next to Trin's ledge and disappeared down the cliff.

Trin listened to the snakeline zing. 'Saved by the bell,' she murmured. She smiled out at the brewing storm. A blast of wind buffeted the cliff face, rattling the storm door against the rock.

THE BELOW

A trail of bubbles gushed upwards as the water pushed the last of the air out of Rilla's lungs. She was pulled down into the darkening blue. As she twisted and struggled to pull free of the painful grip, heat and fear flooded her body. What was this creature? Her muscles tensed, ready to fight to be free before she became food for whatever creature this was.

You must never go up alone. Rilla's heart thumped as Lana's neume blasted into her mind, and her skin turned silty grey with the shock and fear. She twisted once more and was finally able to see Lana, whose skin was glowing the murky crimson of anger.

Lana tugged Rilla downwards and moved to grip her arms, causing fresh, stark pain.

Neeva swam up and pushed in between Rilla and Lana. *Be understanding of your sister*, she neumed to Lana.

Rilla surfaced alone. She broke the rules. Lana flushed a brighter red of indignation. *Everyone knows it's forbidden to visit the Above without an escort.*

She's curious, Lana, reasoned Neeva, rippling a calm green-blue.

Curious about that place. Lana's skin flashed murky yellow, showing her disgust.

You didn't have to go alone, neumed Neeva.

Rilla saw the hint of a smile showing on her sister's face and dared a small smile in return, which Lana noticed and began tugging even harder.

Enough, Lana. Neeva strengthened the message in her neume with a wave of iridescent turquoise that flowed across her skin as she tried to calm her sister. *Stop dragging her. She's doing what you want.*

Lana lessened her grip, but didn't let go.

Rilla strained and turned to face upwards, watching as the sun's rays shone down weakly through the water. The Above suddenly felt so very far away. The warm, bright water of the shallows was gone. It was growing colder, and the water that had felt so benign before now seemed changed. It eddied densely around her, pressing in on her from all sides. There was still the familiarity of the infinite blues, but they looked darker than she recalled.

Now, the rocks and sea plants, the food animals and danger animals all became so many blue shapes blending together in an oppressive, dark blue world.

A great hunger to feast on the colours left behind in the Above rose in Rilla, and her eyes burned to see them again. She felt another tug, and her panicked mind filled with imaginings of the Deeps. Where the blues became black. She shuddered and pushed the frightening darkness from her mind.

She thought again of the Above and the creatures surrounded by so much colour, although there was some colour in Lemuria. Rilla and all the Abrax made colour; it was part of their language. Changes in colours enriched the communication of the neumes, and could sometimes influence mood or occasionally sway a difference in opinion between two Abrax.

Rilla recalled the distant air-words she had heard drifting from the shore, and the walker songs she had added to her choosing song. She always listened carefully, greedily, when she heard those words on the wind. Reaching out with her mind, she had felt those faint neumes and matched them to some of the sounds. She was starting to learn the walker language. Her song had been sung and she was starting to be part of the world of the Above.

Even with such a strong bond forming with the Above, Rilla didn't feel ready to let the Gathering of Colours know about her song, but she would tell them today, if she had to. She had a right to choose, so what could they do?

Her heart darkened along with the water around her as Lana kept tugging her downwards. Rilla pushed the last tiny bubbles of air through her gills and, remembering the wonderful Above, chanced another smile.

The blue darkened further still as they swam through the narrow shaft in the rock and entered Lemuria's cavern. Looking down across the vast space, Rilla could see the multi-coloured luminescence of the Abrax. Countless points of colour were swimming between the spires of the city and around the vast cavern, each Abrax flashing colours in response to shared ideas and feelings in a way that no other creature of the Below could.

I wanted to prepare for my song alone, neumed Rilla. She squirmed again and finally got away from Lana's angry grip.

But that's against the rulings of the Gathering of Colours. Lana yanked at Rilla's arm again.

Lana, enough! Neeva's skin flared, burning orange-red, and she struck Lana in the face. *The Gathering of Colours only recommends that we go with her, Lana. It's Father who's made it law for his daughters.*

I've seen the colours, Neeva, Rilla neumed. *There are so many colours in the Above, more than all our moods and neumes together can conjure. Surely this means there's a place for us up there.*

You're a fool, neumed Lana.

It's just the changeling mind, Neeva neumed to Lana. *Remember? Changelings have such fanciful neumes during their choosing time, and our traditions respect these aberrations, but they don't last.*

I never had such thoughts and desires for the Above, Lana neumed. *I'll tell Father and Mother, and Rilla will be sent to the Deeps so she can have her thoughts redirected.* Lana's skin had darkened to a rage-filled black. She struck Rilla hard on the side of the head, then turned and dived away, her tails whipping the water like angry eels as she swam hard towards the Hall of Colours.

Rilla's eyes stung as they always did when there was pain, but at least Lana's surging anger was fading as the distance between them grew. *I saw them*, Rilla neumed to Neeva once Lana was out of range.

The walkers? Today?

Yes. Rilla was careful not to let her neumes reveal how many times she had crept close to the shore and watched the walkers. *They're so different from us. There are so many different colours all mixed together and other coloured creatures swimming in the sky.* Rilla stopped and drifted, looking at the flickers of colour around the city. *We make such beautiful colours here as well, so surely that's a sign that we should ascend. Creatures with such colour belong in the sun, living on the land, and being part of that world with all its coloured creatures.*

Rilla, hush, your choosing is a time for curiosity and awkward thinking, but such neumes are dangerous, cautioned Neeva.

Why are they dangerous? The right for every Abrax to decide to change and ascend is in the ancient neumes, set in place by the Gathering of Colours. I'm simply considering the ancient decree. Surely considering my right is not dangerous.

Neeva led Rilla to a small rock shelf high on the cavern slopes, away from chance meetings with other Abrax. *The decree was put in place eons ago, Rilla, after all of Mother Ocean and the Above trembled and shook, and the skies grew dark, and the sun didn't show itself for a long and terrible while. If you've learned those lessons, you know the Gathering of Colours was faced by very difficult circumstances. Many creatures suffered and died when the Above blackened.*

I know my lessons, Rilla responded. *I'm not a youngling anymore. The oceans froze over and only the Abrax that descended to the Deeps were safe from the chill of death. The Abrax that went, and the animals that followed, were the only ones to survive.*

They say the blue was black everywhere when the sun was gone, Neeva neumed, *but the Abrax dived deep and glowed together. Their colours kept them brave and strong. The Abrax remained alive when many other creatures perished. They endured those difficulties by staying together, Rilla.* Neeva twined one of her tails with Rilla's. *Together.*

Rilla continued the story. *But some grew to hate the darkness.* She shuddered at the idea of the Abrax, of her, spending time down in the blackness of the Deeps. *So when the Above lightened again, those who couldn't bear even the blue yearned to go up and live in the light. They created the catalyst and debated whether to ascend. The Gathering of Colours wanted the unrest to end, so they voted and the decree was made. Those who decided to go could take the catalyst and ascend to live and walk on the land.*

Yes, continued Neeva. *The diktat was made by the Gathering of Colours, and many decided to ingest the catalyst, to evolve and ascend, to take a place in the light-filled, unknown world of the land. After that time, the Abrax were no longer together.* Neeva's tail tightened around Rilla's. *You're my sister. I don't want us to be apart. I know your thoughts are restless during your deciding, but that'll pass.*

The walkers look so fascinating. Rilla was staring upward. *And they do such interesting things.*

So you saw them today?

No. Yes. Rilla's secret slipped from its hiding place in her mind, and images of the Above flooded into her neume before she could stop them.

It wasn't just today. How many times? Neeva's tails stiffened.

Many.

Rilla! What were you thinking?

Rilla stared at her sister and smiled broadly, rippling bands of violet and lavender elation flowing across her skin. She reached with her mind to ensure no other Abrax was close and then let her neumes of wonder and curiosity pour out, sharing the amazing wonders she'd seen when she'd dared to venture close to the walkers' world.

You can't neume these things about the Above, Rilla. Father will be angry enough that you've broken his laws. If he finds out your thoughts, who knows what he'll do.

Rilla's skin paled to yellow.

Neeva smiled and untangled her tails from Rilla's. *We need go to Father now and try to undo the damage Lana's angry neumes may have caused.*

THE ABOVE

Station policy mandated that when the storm siren sounded, all personnel had to go directly to their designated sleeping quarters, or a secure work area, and log in by scanning their ID bracelets. The bracelets could not be removed. This was a failsafe policy, ensuring that whoever was monitoring from the control centre would know that everyone was in an area where they could be sealed in before the storm surge pounded up against the escarpment.

Sharly had only just gotten to the bottom of the lowest ladder and was starting to climb as Meg unclipped from the snake next to her. Meg looked out at the storm and called something to Sharly that was lost in the wind. Then she jogged off along the rock ledge towards the control centre.

Trin knew there was no rush to close the storm seal. There was time for Sharly to reach the cave, just enough time, just … She remained where she had been sitting at the cave entrance and watched her friend climb, enjoying the feeling of the storm building. The energy of the ions in the air made her skin prickle, and the spectacle of the sea, whipped into a frenzy by the blustering winds, captivated her.

She sat perched on the very edge to be as close to the storm as she could get, feeling the ocean surge and pull back like a drawn-in breath, watching as the water swelled and flooded over the rock ledge before retreating as though it was running to hide somewhere before forcing itself across the rocks again. Her breath had slowed and fallen into rhythm with the surging of the sea. Its energy surrounded her until she could hardly notice anything else.

Then there was that *something* again. It was the same sensation she had *heard-felt* when she was in the sea earlier, but now the signal was less urgent. Now this thing was signalling a whispered, burbling concern. It made no sense to her, but it felt like something was out there, mixed up with the sea.

Trin shook her head to clear away the whispers, and concentrated instead on the thunder as it drummed across the grey, boiling sky, which was being cut with knives of lightning. With each flare, Trin could see the angry water mountaining up all the way to the horizon.

'The waves are huge,' she called over the edge to Sharly, 'the big surge isn't far off.'

With the next bright bolt of lightning, Trin saw the wall of water heading straight at the station. 'Just enough time,' she whispered. 'I hope.'

She leaned out again to check on her friend's progress, and as she did, she unclipped the domed storm shield. It rattled on its hinges and creaked as it strained against the wind.

Sharly reached the top of the ladder. Trin grabbed her by the harness and pulled her inside, then scanned her own wristband across the sensor on the wall. Sharly was struggling to sit up, so Trin grabbed her arm and tapped her band on the scanner. There was a green acknowledge signal from control.

More lightning, and Trin could see that the wave was now a cliff of water. It would be only moments before it slammed into the real cliff that was Whitlam Station. Home. The sucking, growling sound of the angry sea echoed off the cave walls, making the air shudder and pound on their eardrums.

Control would throw the failsafe door switch soon, but Trin always liked to make sure she closed the door herself. She wanted Meg and Dad to see that she and Sharly deserved the trust and independence of having their own digs. Trin took a last breath of the zinging ion-rich air and hit the initiate switch. The domed, carbon-glass storm shield hissed into position and sealed against the locking ring that encircled the cave entrance. Everything was suddenly quiet, then the dome groaned as the wall of water slammed into the station.

Sharly and Trin sat close together in the dark, listening to the roaring, angry sea-beast pounding against the door. Sharly didn't switch on the lights, knowing Trin liked to see the storm as it was, not hide behind the comforts of tech. So it was there in the dark that Sharly noticed her friend's skin.

'Weirdness. You're glowing. What's that about?' blurted Sharly, touching Trin's arm.

'I haven't had a shower yet since fishing,' Trin stammered. 'I must've swum through a bloom that was luminescent. That's what Meg said it was, anyway,' she added as an afterthought.

'That's crankin', Trin. I must've had it, too. If I hadn't washed mine off, then we could've had a mad light show.'

Sitting in the dark, Trin stared out at the storm, thinking. If she couldn't tell Sharly, who could she tell? She rubbed her hand along her arm. 'It's not a bloom, Sharly. Somehow … it's me,' she mumbled.

'You glow? Come on, Trin girl, isn't talking to the fish enough weird for you?'

Trin took a trembling breath. 'I don't know what it is.'

'Unshackle, Trin, it might not be algae, but it could be something else, something from the sea, like pollution, you know, or maybe you're sick.'

'Not you, too. Cut back, Sharls. Enough of the sick thing, okay?'

'Sorry, Trin.' Sharly squeezed Trin's hands. 'Unshackle, girl. Whatever it is, I'll help you figure it out.'

'Thanks, Sharls. I know lots of things have changed out there since the rising, but maybe new things are happening, too, that we haven't discovered yet. Maybe whatever it is that's doing this is like an allergy or something. I might be part of a great discovery,' said Trin, trying to make herself feel less dismayed.

Sharly rubbed Trin's arm. 'It's fading now.'

'You're a good friend,' said Trin. 'Thanks for not making me seem weird or sick.' Suddenly she needed to tell Sharly everything. 'Do you believe I can sense the fish, Sharly?'

'Yeah, if you say so.' Sharly placed her arm around Trin's shoulders. 'I've known you forever and you've never lied to me. And we'd never caught so many fish before you started with the fish-talk thing. Sorry, I know you hate it when Tennan calls it that. He's a frube.'

Trin lifted her still slightly glowing arm. 'But look … it might not just be the fish-talk.' She sighed. 'I can hear other things out there, too, and I think they're getting louder.'

'Like what?'

'I don't know how to describe it. The signals are getting more intense, like this skill I have is getting stronger and ...'

'And what?'

'I think I'm actually controlling what the fish do now. I tried it today, making the fish come to the nets, and I knew when the sharks were coming.'

Sharly flicked on the light and glared at her. 'So if you knew the sharks were coming, why did you stay in the water?'

'To give you guys a chance to get to safety.'

'Well, thanks, but how dumb are you? The sharks would find you just as edible as any of us.'

'But they *didn't* eat me. I made them focus on the school and not me, then I ... told them to chase the school back out to sea. I showed them, anyway.'

'What made you think that being alone in the water, surrounded by sharks, was a great time to run an experiment? What if you'd been wrong?' Sharly sighed. She looked questioning, doubtful. 'It was probably luck, Trin, a fluke.'

'But, Sharls, I could *feel* it. It's real.' Trin wasn't sure whether she was trying to convince Sharly or herself.

'How long have you thought you could do this?' asked Sharly without a hint of judgment.

'You know I've been able to sense where to find the fish for a few weeks, since back around Raz's birthday, when the weather was colder and the fish were less active.'

'And we hadn't caught anything for ages,' Sharly added. 'I remember our unusual good luck.'

'Yeah, when that school showed up I was so worried they'd change direction. I was hoping they'd keep moving to the nets. Then they faltered and turned. Then I was really hoping and wishing they'd turn back and suddenly they did. I had such a strange feeling that day. I was sure I'd made them move toward the nets. I tried it again the next time and I've been experimenting. I can do it every time now.'

'Well, I have to say that it seems like the fish have been tripping over our nets since you've been doing your fish-control thing. But what about today, when those sharks came at you? It didn't look like you had control of *them*.'

'I made them come towards me.'

'And you didn't think to bail out?'

Trin ignored the question. She had to say all this now, before she lost her nerve. 'I was scared the sharks would come after you guys, so I made an illusion … well, I think I did. I imagined a school of fish all around me, and the sharks turned towards me, swimming around looking for the fish. I could feel them sliding past me. It was terrifying.'

'And you think you controlled them?'

'I *believe* I did.'

'And then you made a message to send them away again?'

'No.' Trin stared at Sharly's reflection in the dome. 'I froze. I could barely keep up my illusion of the school.'

'So what happened?'

'I felt something else, another ... something.' Trin shrugged. 'Then I sensed a new school further out to sea, and the sharks turned towards it, but it wasn't me that did it. Maybe that was where the rest of the real school had ended up. There was another thing, Sharly.'

'Do tell.'

'After the sharks left, there was like a voice, in my head, or at least a feeling ... of relief, like someone was glad I was safe.'

'Too weird.'

'Sharly, what's happening to me?' Trin rubbed her clammy pale hands together.

'Maybe you're right, and you're reacting to some new thing in the water that we haven't discovered yet. You could ask your dad.'

'No way, you saw how he reacted today. He's always worrying about me getting sick. No, I need to find out some other way.'

'It might just all be a coincidence, Trin. Maybe it's nothing.'

'It's not nothing.' Trin snapped. 'You think I'm making it all up.'

'Hey, girl, I believe you.' Sharly took her by the hands. 'I don't know what's going on, but I'll help you find out.'

THE BELOW

What were you thinking? Why did you go alone? It's forbidden! Father raged. His skin flickered black and muddy green, then darkest red, to reinforce the menacing indignation of his neume.

Rilla felt the pressure of her father's anger inside her head, pulsing in painful waves. When each wave withdrew, her mind was left in a black fog of dizzying dread. She wanted to regurgitate, but would not let herself weaken and do such a disrespectful thing in the Hall of Colours with the members of the Gathering watching. Her stomach rose and she swallowed hard, clenching her teeth. She stared down at her greying tails and watched the translucent fins spasm each time Father's angry neumes struck.

We know all too well what those walking monsters have done to the Abrax with their ignorant selfish ways, Father seethed. *Because of their adulteration, Mother Ocean is being poisoned and warmed. In the north and south of the planet, the ice is melting, sending flooding torrents into our beautiful world. This inundation diminishes the brine and causes the fish to bloat and die. We can no longer trust the currents. The shallows are now ravaged by storms and are no longer havens for the fishes to breed and replenish their numbers. What possessed you, Rilla, to surface alone, and to go so near the shore and those abhorrent walkers?*

Rilla buried her desire for the Above deep inside her mind before she dared respond. *It was a lapse, Father. I was excited and acted impulsively.* She made her skin a humble blue to reinforce the neume of contrition and respect.

I can't have the Gathering of Colours seeing one of my daughters as a lawbreaker.

Thal, she is not a law breaker, Rilla's mother neumed as she floated up by his side to soothe him. *The members of the Gathering see the good work you do for the Abrax and Lemuria. They also understand how excited a changeling gets when it's their choosing time and they're preparing to sing their choice.*

You don't understand, Ula. Father was trembling.

I understand that Rilla is young, and that you are kind and wise. Mother curled a tail around one of Father's. *And you are loving, Thal.*

Rilla watched her father's dark, angry glow fade to crimson to match her mother's. After a long moment, he neumed, *You have one more chance, Rilla. You're forbidden to go to the surface alone. One of us must go with you every time you visit the Above while you prepare to sing your choosing in two moons. Sometimes the newly grown are headstrong, so you need to be reminded that you are Abrax and don't belong in the world of the Above.*

Rilla took an extra tight grip on her thoughts to ensure that her father couldn't sense she had already made her choice. She wanted to argue, to complain about Lana's cruelty, but Neeva's tail coiled around her own and squeezed a warning.

Thank you, Father, Rilla neumed, making her skin turn pink. *Humility—love.*

Neeva, Lana, watch over your sister, Thal neumed.

We will, neumed Neeva, as she guided Rilla away.

Rilla felt a shove from behind and knew it was Lana. *If Father catches you surfacing alone again, you'll be sent to the Deeps to become hissi-weed.*

Mind your neumes, Lana, scolded Neeva. *How could you hope for such a dark and horrid fate to befall your sister? Besides, hissi-weed is just an old witching tale.*

Rilla's mind filled with flashes of the many tales of the Deeps neumed to all the younglings of Lemuria. The Deeps was where the Abrax had sheltered during the time of the long dark sky. The catalyst that could change Abrax to walkers had been made down there. The old witching tales described a strange, amazing and magical place in the reaches of the Deeps.

A tale flooded into her mind and she neumed to her sisters. *In the deepest of the Deeps there's an enchanted garden filled with strange plants, cultivated by the sea-witch. The witch tends her exotic kelps, giant sponges and dancing anemones with the help of ancient magic. She makes things grow down there that have no reason or capacity to grow, except for the witch's powerful conjuring.*

Neeva took over from Rilla and continued. *The garden is said to be radiant, and the plants so huge and vibrant that they light up the Deeps. Special plants that only grow there were harvested and blended to make the catalyst, so the sea-witch keeps her garden hidden and secret, and protected inside a strong enchantment.*

That's not where the story ends, neumed Lana.

Rilla cringed at the reminder of a darker and more ominous tale that was neumed to all younglings as their choosing grew close.

The crone works other, necessary magic for the good of the Abrax, insisted Lana. *In her garden, dispersed between those wonders of the Deeps, the old witch deals*

65

with the banished—the lawbreakers of Lemuria. She plants them into the magical soil of the Deeps, where they take root and grow into half-thinking hissi-weed. To remain there in the sea-witch's garden for eternity so they can do no more harm to the Abrax.

Rilla shivered. Those were just tales to scare younglings into not straying too far from the city or its rules, and I'm no longer a youngling.

But the Deeps are real, neumed Lana. I've neumed with the guards that Father has sent down to escort Abrax to the witch. They never bring them back.

Cease your cruelness, Lana, this is all foolish blather. Neeva pulled Rilla away, neuming her with a wave of comfort.

The two sisters swam together back to their nest far above the city. Floating near the nest, coiled together, they looked back down through the blue to the glowing Hall of Colours in the centre of the city. Intricately husbanded coral palaces and gardens spread out in all directions from the great hall, the coral creeping up the slopes of the immense cavern. They watched the school of Abrax moving in and around the coral spires and rambling gardens. The luminescence of each Abrax shimmered and flickered as their individual ideas and feelings added to the beauty of the ever-changing city.

The scene was glorious, but Rilla couldn't stop thinking of the strange amazements she had seen in the Above.

Is it true about the Deeps, Neeva? Are they real? Rilla's skin faded to grey-yellow.

Lana's right about the Deeps, Neeva neumed. *It's more than just the old tales, but I know very little, unlike Lana with her sly ways of finding things out.*

I don't want to be sent there. Rilla paled further.

You won't be sent anywhere just for being curious, little sister.

Rilla gazed around to ensure they were alone. *But, Neeva, I'm more than curious. I want to ascend. I believe I can help heal Mother Ocean. If the Abrax and the walkers combined their knowledge we could hasten the healing and that would help us all.*

Your ideas about helping with the healing are unselfish. Neeva smiled and squeezed her sister's tail in her own. *Your thoughts about the Above are stronger than I've felt from you before, but the way you're feeling is part of your choosing time. It'll pass. When it was my time to decide and I pondered the Above, it helped me to fill my mind with thoughts of Lemuria.* She flicked her free tail and they turned so that Rilla was looking over the city again.

Regardless of the beauty of Lemuria, and the purity of the neume and the mind songs the Abrax shared, Rilla's mind remained filled with images of the Above, with its colourful multiplicity, the fascinating air-words, and the walkers who spoke and sang them. Why wasn't this life in the Below enough for her?

Regardless of the two moon cycles remaining until Rilla's choosing ceremony, she had made her decision. Soon she would have to neume her sister and parents, telling them that she had chosen to take the catalyst and ascend.

THE ABOVE

In the morning, the storm was long gone, the only signs of its passing the huge glossy mounds of kelp that had been flung up all along the rock shelf, and the strong arrhythmic swell that always jostled the ocean in a storm's wake.

Trin hit the switch for the storm door. The seal hissed as it released, and the dome swung away, locking back into place against the cliff face.

She sat on the ledge, looking out across the sparkling, jittery water. Her eyes and thoughts were drawn towards Lighthouse Island. All kinds of flotsam had been washed across the island during the storm, but at the centre of the mess, the lighthouse still stood, having survived another storm. This stubborn relic had been part of the landscape since before the rising, though Lighthouse Island had not always been an island.

On the old maps, the island had been the end point of a rocky peninsula that stretched from the ridge of cliffs that had been drilled out to make Whitlam Station, and out to the headland where the lighthouse stood. When the sea levels were lower, clusters of jagged rocks had lain just under the water all around that headland. The lighthouse was a vestige from an even earlier time, before satellite navigation, when its rhythmic strobing light warned ships away from the danger of the hidden rocks.

Now the lighthouse stood stubbornly against the elements, cut off from the mainland as the rising water had swallowed parts of peninsula, just as it had swallowed coastlines all around the world.

Trin thought of the many times the fishers had challenged each other to go to the island, although it was mostly Tennan and Raz.

'I dare you to swim out there, frube.'

'You first, burley for brains.'

The two took turns throwing the dare around, but everyone else ignored them.

'It would be like swimming through a milkshake that's still in the blender,' Mal said once.

The name 'blender' stuck, and that's how everyone referred to the perilous, ripping current that surged through the passage between the station and the island.

Trin was a strong swimmer, probably the strongest of all the fishers, but she had never wanted to go to the island badly enough to take the risk. But lately she found herself thinking about it more and more. She felt there was something to discover over there, but she shrugged the feeling off when it came. With all the *signals* she was receiving in her head, she couldn't trust what was real. She couldn't fathom how *any* of it could be real.

When she gave into her imagination, she had such strong feelings that there was someone over on the island looking at the station. As if, she told herself. She knew that one storm surge would take care of any sly shubee faker that might be hanging out on Lighthouse Island.

There it was again, that feeling of being watched. She shivered and a fresh urge to go to the island blossomed in her mind.

'What are you thinking, girl?' she muttered. Her dad would never let her go back in the water again if he caught her swimming the blender. She shook her head to clear the stupid idea from her mind.

'First sign of madness,' came Sharly's voice from behind her.

'Huh?'

'Talking to yourself while you stare out at that island, *again*.'

'Cut back, Sharls. I just wonder what it's like over there.'

'Well, stop wondering about that, and start wondering about disking,'

'Crankin',' said Trin, refocusing on the water. 'The swell's perfect.' All thoughts of the island vaporised. 'I'll snake down and let everyone know it's on.'

'I'll go and scrounge something for breakfast and meet you all at the Funnel.'

They didn't want to wait for a regular breakfast in the station's dining hall. As soon as the adults had discovered that the fishers had invented disking, they had instantly and very strongly frowned upon it, so it was better to get the competition started and finished before anyone else woke up. The fishers mostly got away with it unless someone got hurt enough to need to be patched up by Meg.

The funnel was a V-shaped formation that narrowed into a long channel between two walls of rock. Massive plumes gushed skyward as the waves were forced to the end of the narrow corridor. With closed eyes, it was easy to imagine the water sounding like an angry dog, growling as it ran along the sides of the long corridor before letting out a loud, blasting *WOOF* as the water was forced upwards when it smashed into the dead end where the channel stopped at a smooth ledge of rock.

For the fishers, the force of the waves rocketing along the Funnel called out to be challenged, so *disking* was invented, helped by a lot of inspiration found in Mal's grandfather's old movies and journals.

They were captivated by the movies and memories describing surfing and the way things were at the beaches before the rising had washed everything away, and inspired by the grainy old footage of massive planks of wood being ridden by singing surfers inside howling tubes of blue water.

Trin had enjoyed watching the funny and inspirational vid-files, and listening as Mal read aloud his grandpa's precious memories about the beach. She knew that just out from the station, below the water, was the slope of the old shoreline, but the last sand had washed away from the last beach when her father was very young. Mal's granddad had lit a fire inside him, and Trin had been caught in that fire's sparks. Mal had come to her and shared his ideas about figuring out a way to *surf*. The thrill of commanding the ocean, even for a brief, hurtling moment, also excited Trin.

'There aren't any beaches anymore,' Mal had told her. 'Well, no sand anyway, but if we watch the swell and time it right we could ride the waves that roll up the Funnel. Then we could land on the ledge at the end.' He had stopped and shaken his head. 'But we don't have boards, and even if we did, wood and fibreglass would never be tough enough to stand up to being bashed against the rocks.'

'We could use the spare storm shields,' suggested Trin. 'They're not flat, but they'd float fine. If they're tough enough for storm surges they'll handle landing on the rock. We could surf in on those.'

Mal was grinning his head off. 'Not surfing … disking!'

Trin could almost feel the rhythm of the waves inside her. 'I'll win,' she teased.

'Cut back, Trin. Surfing's in my blood.'

So the fishers had set up the rules for the disking competition, and made plans to acquire a spare storm shield from storage without anyone noticing it had gone. Then disking was added to the list of things the fishers bent the station rules about.

WOOF! The waves were roaring up the Funnel as the fishers gathered, staring out at the water as they ate their scavenged breakfast. They were already dressed in their thick winter wetskins, which offered extra protection.

They all knew it was important to spend time paying attention to the rhythm of the sea before they attempted a run. They had to pick the wave that would speed them down the Funnel, and then lift them and the disk onto the rock ledge. No one wanted to be stuck riding a *howler*—a wave that didn't lift but instead slammed down into the front of the ledge. As the wave pummelled the rock, it would make a woofing, howling sound, and so would the person riding it as they, and the disk, were flung up into the air when the water blasted against the rock.

The team always stuck together. There were always a few fishers waiting with the fishing net ready to catch whoever became an airborne howler before they landed on the rock. Well, usually anyway.

As an acknowledgement of his genius for inventing disking, Mal was always the one to take the first run. Now he hefted the disk onto his shoulder and headed up to the end of the narrow ledge at the mouth of the Funnel. He waited, watching, then bellyflopped onto the disk and into the peak of the swell as it started to pull back out. Then he paddled around to wait for his wave. Everyone stood watching, loudly speculating with each other about which wave he would choose.

Leaning over the edge of the disk, Mal started paddling like a machine. His weight made one side of the disk dip down low in the water. The other side stuck up high, catching the curling slope of the incoming wave. Now the disk was picking up speed and Mal needed to decide what degree of difficulty he would choose—stay kneeling, squat or stand.

The fishers had come up with only these three degrees of difficulty so far. They had thought of plenty of stunts that could be designated for a fourth level, but they also predicted that any of those would result in certain maiming, so three levels would have to do.

Mal was on his knees, then standing with his hands up in the air. 'Cowabunga!' he screamed, like he always did in honour of his granddad.

The wave growled ominously. Maybe Mal had picked a howler by mistake. Holding one side of the fishing net,

Trin took a firmer grip and started concentrating on which place on the rock ledge Mal was likely to land if the wave did turn into a howler.

Mal grinned with confidence as he rode. He saw Trin lift the net and started shaking his head, wet ropes of hair flopping around his face. He raised a finger, waggled it and mouthed, *No-no-no*.

The wave surged down the Funnel. Mal was only metres from the ledge, and lift. The wave stopped its growling and flopped up onto the ledge. Mal pushed down on one side of the disk as he skimmed across the rocks, carried on the last ribbons of the water. His push made the disk spin a half-turn as it came to a stop.

Everyone cheered.

'Degree of difficulty three, and an original landing,' called Trin. 'Kudos!'

As soon as Mal stepped off the disk, Tennan grabbed it and sprinted along the ledge.

'He's rushing it,' said Nix.

'He does that,' said Mal quietly.

'I bet you he howls,' said Sharly.

'So who's willing to bet he doesn't?' Trin asked.

'I'll get the net,' said Raz.

Tennan made screeching, seagull noises as he flew up into the air at the end of his run, but he did manage an impressive double somersault before he was caught in the net, so he scored some points.

It was Trin's turn. She lifted the disk onto her shoulder and walked along the ledge. She stepped quietly, taking her time until her feet fell into the rhythm of the wave patterns. *Three waves and then a howl, seven, then another howl, four, then a third, and then it repeats.* The rhythm moved from her feet to her heart, and by the time she reached the push-off point she didn't need to hesitate. She swung the disk from her shoulder and let its weight pull her into the swell.

'Thank you,' she said quietly to the sea as she paddled out. 'Thank you for sharing the secret of your rhythm with me.'

The wave moved in. Trin leaned over the front of the disk and pulled through the water to get into position. This wave was fast. She paddled hard, leaning further forward, trying to stay ahead of the wave. She hoped she hadn't gotten it all wrong. The force of the water tilted the disk and Trin feared she would be bucked out. She leaned her weight back and urged the low side of the disk back up. Then she took a breath, squatted and stood. She looked towards the ledge, glad to see the net hanging from Mal's hands.

The wave was moving so fast now that the growl had become a whining hiss. The wave pushed her on. She was halfway down the Funnel when she leaned back, rebalancing, as the force of the wave tilted the disk forward again. When she was three-quarters of the way down the Funnel, the water level dipped.

Trin knew this wave wouldn't howl. Maybe she could try something special.

She leaned her weight on one side of the disk, and it twisted around. Then she moved her weight the other way, and the disk twisted again. It worked. She was starting to spin as she approached the ledge. Only metres now. She spun around again. The rock was closer.

'Lift,' she said to the wave. The wave was taking its time. She spun around again. 'Lift.'

Then she felt the force, pushing up under the disk. Up she went, leaning into the disk to make it spin faster as she floated across the ledge. It grated on the rock as the water flowed away. The spinning slowed, but before it stopped she tilted the disk and stepped out as though she was a movie star from the olden days, stepping from a limo onto the red carpet.

'Degree of difficulty … four?' Mal questioned the team.

They all nodded. Trin bowed.

'Ladies and jellyfish, we have a first.' Everyone cheered and crushed Trin in an octopus hug, with too many arms and legs. She could barely breathe, but she didn't care. She held the new top score.

Sharly, Nix and Raz all scored a three before they had to stop the competition because people were up and about at the station.

Tennan got the low scorer's privilege of hiding the gear, and then they all went in search of a real breakfast in the dining hall.

THE BELOW

Thal had demanded that Lana and Neeva watch over Rilla, and accompany her whenever she went to the Above. Lana was so hateful about the idea that she never did, but Neeva often went with Rilla to float together on the warm currents. She always insisted that they stay away from the shallows and the walkers, which meant they could only watch the birds swimming in the sky rather than the fascinating creatures walking on the shore.

They had made these visits to the Above together many times since the last moon, but Neeva had her own preoccupations and couldn't always watch Rilla.

Rilla did wonder if Neeva sometimes saw her drift away on her own, but sensed her sister's yearning and said nothing. So, since promising her father not to surface alone, Rilla had broken her promise many times.

When Rilla went to the Above alone, she swam a little closer to the shore each time. One time she swam, fascinated, through the deserted remnants of the drowned walker city that had been left twisted and rotting when the seas had risen and swallowed the land. The city was far bigger than the walker nests she had seen on the shore. The ruins lay faded, warped and collapsing, held in place by a crust of anemones and barnacles that clung to the wreckage. She thought they may have been meeting places once, but now forests of kelp grew between them.

Rilla wondered what the walkers had done in this place before it was washed away. It was big enough to welcome many walkers. Where could they all have gone? Did they yearn for this place? She flitted through the flooded walker world, feasting on the oddity.

Pushing through a copse of tall kelp, she saw a walker's face staring at her. *Danger!*

Rilla twisted and darted away to hide, crashing into a barnacled wall that was concealed by the kelp. Her fin pained; it had been ripped. Her eyes burned with the discomfort. Her heart drummed and her gills gulped. She turned to see if the walker had followed her.

There was nothing there.

She crept out from the kelp, her fin throbbing. The walker was still lying where she had seen it. It was much smaller than others she had seen. It wasn't moving. She drifted closer. Still it didn't move. It stared at her.

Perhaps it's dead. She reached to touch it. Lifted it. It didn't have the softness of a dead thing. It felt rigid like coral, but smooth. A barnacle was attached to it, a large bump on the head of this miniature walker. Her heart slowed and her curiosity returned. She looked at where the smooth walker had been and saw other smooth, colourful things there, also covered with barnacles. So much strangeness.

She took the miniature walker with her and swam away from the shoreline before coming to the surface. The water was warm and Rilla floated in the gentle swell, relishing the freedom. The walker lay on her chest as she stared up into the sky and rubbed its smooth, round head. The pale head reminded her of the moon, which was growing round again.

When the moon next became full in the sky, all the Abrax would gather for her choosing ceremony. Rilla shuddered at the thought of her father's reaction when she declared that she wished to ascend.

But choosing is my right.

Her mother and Neeva would be pale with sadness and shock.

No! Nothing will make me change my mind. This world is what I want.

She ran her hand over the smooth, tiny walker and drew in a long breath. The air was filled with all the tantalising and unfamiliar smells of the Above. The seabirds squawked and jostled each other as they criss-crossed the piercing blue sky. In the distance she saw the people of the Above walking to and fro on the rocky edge of the land. They looked so stiff compared to the constant flowing movements of the Abrax.

It was hard to believe the walkers had really come from the sea. So long ago, in the time of the Great Choosing, many Abrax had taken the catalyst and come to live on the land. These stiff, walking creatures were their descendants.

Rilla and the other younglings had studied the drowned skeletons of walkers and compared them to the bones of dead Abrax. The walkers and the Abrax had the corporeal in common. Underneath their different skins, they had common bones: arms that ended with fingers, and legs that ended with toes, even if, in the case of the Abrax, those toes were concealed within fins. Both Abrax and walkers had muscles for smiling and frowning, and lungs for either gulping through gills or breathing the thin, sun-filled air. The changes that transformed the Abrax to walker only happened because of the catalyst, but those changes were still, for the most part, only skin deep.

There had been stories, old tales passed down through the generations, about the catalyst sometimes failing and turning from a wonder into a curse. Sometimes, when there was only a partial change, a changeling would remain half Abrax and half walker, and be stuck somewhere between worlds, belonging in neither.

Rilla wondered now if the purpose of those horrible lessons and stories was to plant fear deep into the younglings' minds so they would be filled with dread, ensuring they would stay unchanged and remain in the Below.

More recently, the younglings were also schooled about the ugliness that the walkers had inflicted on the land, and how their actions were now poisoning the fish, warming the seas, and threatening to kill Mother Ocean. Rilla believed, more strongly than ever, that the remedy for both worlds was for the Abrax and walkers to work together, to share their knowledge and unite their efforts to heal the damage. But she could not imagine that her father, or the Gathering of Colours, would ever consider such unification.

Rilla glided in close to the shallows, until she could easily see every detail of the walkers. Their golden-brown, unchanging skin was decorated with coverings and ornaments. She had learned that, instead of sharing emotion colours as the Abrax did, the walkers communicated ideas and feelings through a fascinating collection of sounds. They chattered and sang like happy dolphins, and they bellowed and moaned like whales when they were troubled.

Rilla had watched and listened, spellbound by the strangeness. She listened to the air-sounds the walkers made and mimicked them. Now that she had breathed air, she was hungry to learn the walkers' air-language.

She sensed soft neumes. Some walkers still possessed a slight ability to neume, so she could feel the wispy thoughts they sent without them even knowing they possessed the ability. Listening carefully, and matching the neumes to the air-words she heard, she had learned the walker language quickly.

She now understood that it wasn't the entire population of walkers that had done the damage to Earth and caused Mother Ocean to be poisoned, although many walkers had been willing to ignore the problems. She admired their strength and spirit and, regardless of Father and attempts by the Gathering of Colours to make the walkers appear as monsters, Rilla's affections for them grew, particularly for the one called Marcus.

The sun had risen high in the sky while Rilla had floated and watched, and now she had lost the advantage of the shadow that she hid in at the shoreline. She reluctantly moved back into the deeper water and floated just below the surface, in the warm current. Still holding the small walker by its tiny smooth hand, she drifted, stretching her arms out wide and closing her eyes. The sunlight refracted through the water and played dancing patterns of light across her eyelids.

Thoughts about the walkers filled her head. How different they were from the teachings she had been encouraged to believe. And Marcus, he was no monster. He neumed strongly, and she had seen his hopes and dreams. His thoughts were always focused on ways of healing the sea.

Far off in the distance, she heard an unexpected noise, harsh and frantic. Rilla startled, and the tiny walker slipped from her hand. The small, round face stared up at her as it drifted downwards into the blue.

The noise was coming from the direction of the walkers' nests on the shore and was moving toward her. It clattered like the calls of the petrels heading home to their mates in the high rocky roosts as the day ended.

The clattering noise drew closer. Rilla could feel the agitation of the water all around her as it synchronised with the noise. She sunk down deeper to observe the noisy intrusion from a safe distance.

She had seen these noisy things before. They were help-animals the walkers used to move on the water now that they no longer had fins. When Rilla had neumed about this noisy creature to her sister, Neeva had neumed *boat* in response.

From below, Rilla watched as the dark shape moved across the glittering scales of light on the water's surface above. She could see the source of the commotion; the tail of the bulbous floating boat creature hung down into the water. Its fin was beating in the water rapidly, as if it was fleeing from a danger animal. The boat's noisy fin churned the water and created an explosion of bubbles in its wake, then it suddenly fell silent. The boat stopped and drifted on the current.

Rilla held still, hiding herself in the column of shadow cast down through the water below the boat. Without warning, the boat regurgitated a large dark object that plummeted past her, grazing Rilla's uninjured tail. Her skin darkened to black-purple with the shock of it and her eyes stung in response to the pain. She let herself float upwards, then lay under the belly of the boat as she rubbed the tender welt on her tail.

Once the pain had faded, Rilla became aware of a muffled sound coming from the boat. She fizzed with excitement as she realised the walkers were talking. Quieting herself, she reached out, feeling for any trace of a neume. Maybe these walkers were some of those that still issued neumes when they exchanged air-words with each other.

A faint neumed green of concern came with the air-words that mumbled through the water. There was no black anger in the green, so Rilla took the chance to go closer and listen. Keeping her body pressed to the curve of the boat's belly, she dared to raise her ears out of the water. She was excited; the words were so much louder and clearer now than when she had heard them blown on the breeze.

She recognised a familiar neume; he was here! Marcus was here, in the boat above her. She was so mesmerised by the overwhelming joy of having him so close that she forgot to breathe, or gulp. Curling herself close under the bulging side of the boat, struggling to suppress the bubbles that fizzed through her gills, she tried to hold her happiness in check. She calmed herself and stayed pressed hard up against the boat, where she could listen without being seen.

'Salinity levels are still dropping, Marcus. In some places it's under twenty-eight parts per thousand.'

'There'll be massive species die-off soon, with those numbers.' The walker, Marcus, said, neuming heavy-green concern and yellow fear. 'The fish will try to match their internal salinity to their environment. No species can adapt fast enough to survive the bloat if the seas get any fresher. All we can do is watch, and take note of the strongest and most adaptable species. Then we'll try to collect some and send them to Mawson Station, or the aquarium at High and Dry for a controlled-breeding program. Then we might have something to release back into the sea if a serious die-off does happen.'

'We need to keep watching and collect as many viable adults as we can.'

'You're right, Jasper, but with all the storms, it's like trying to find scaly needles in a very wet and angry haystack. All we can do is try to get out with the nets as often as we can between the storm surges, and capture as much breeding stock as we can and move them into tanks with salinity controlled at thirty-five ppt. The theory from Mawson is that if we bring the salinity down slowly, and keep our fingers crossed and hope, the fish will adapt to the new salinity levels and breed adapted offspring.'

Marcus neumed *frustration—doubt*. 'We just need to know where the fish are hangin' out, my friend.'

I know where the fish are. Rilla's skin glowed pink. *I could easily show the walkers where to find them, Marcus*.

'Here, fishy-fishy,' said Jasper.

Marcus and Jasper both made the mysterious huffing noise Rilla had wondered about. She matched this noise with neumes, and now realised it was the noise that walkers made when they were happy; it was laughter. The neumes she felt from them were of frustration mixed with happiness. This combination of feelings confounded her. How could they be feeling so frustrated but make laughter?

Abrax could have private feelings while sharing public neumes, but there was always a coalescence of the two states of thought, not opposition. Perhaps, when the walkers lost their ability to neume, their minds altered in other ways.

Rilla pushed these analytical ideas aside, preferring to listen to the Marcus walker's tuneful voice. Her heart fluttered as she listened to him talking. The long tresses of the cirrus on her head and around her gird prickled with excitement. Her skin glowed pink-crimson.

Marcus cared about her world; he didn't want it destroyed any more than the Abrax did. She felt the strength of the neume of his concern, and his dedication to the healing, and this filled her with the courage to face Father and declare her choice.

Something wrapped around Rilla's gird. It squeezed her tightly, forcing all of her forbidden breath from her. She looked down at something dark that was coiling around her. Kraken. No, they were never in the shallows.

Not a kraken, sister. Lana's face twisted into view, blackened with anger, as was the rest of her. *This is much worse than a kraken, Rilla, or it will be when I tell Father you broke your promise.*

THE ABOVE

It was a sure thing; as sure as high tide followed low tide. After the fishers had brought in a huge catch of fish, scaled them and cleaned them, there were huge piles of fish guts that needed to be hauled up the cliffs to the gardens at the top.

Up at the gardens, the biotechs would take the fish innards and combine them with other composted garden waste, vegetable scraps and human waste. Then they waved a scientific magic wand over it all and eventually the stinking goop would turn into high-grade fertiliser.

Without fertiliser, it would have been next to impossible to grow any food on the cliff tops. The meagre local soil was leached of goodness by storm run-off, and it was a little too salty. Adding the custom-made fertiliser supercharged the depleted dirt into an amazing growing medium. This effort allowed the station to keep its staff and their families well fed without wasting time, credits and resources trekking back and forth to High and Dry to pick up supplies.

Now that the disking competition and bragging was over, and the fishers had washed the salt from themselves and their wetskins, and then had another breakfast, it was time to move the guts they had pulled out of yesterday's catch up the ladders to the gardens.

Life was mostly vertical at Whitlam Station. There was work at the base of the escarpment, in the labs and in the water, and more work up on top, in the gardens. Everything in between the two involved traversing the cliffs, up the ladders and down the snakes. Without a harness to attach to the rope for abseiling down a snake, there was no choice but to come back down the ladders. This was slow and much less fun. Besides, people needed to move fast if a storm siren sounded, so no one went anywhere, except into the water, without their harness on.

Moving loads vertically was essential but challenging work. The harnesses had been modified over time and fitted with load hooks, which enabled tough cargo

91

boxes, made from lightweight recycled plastics, to be hooked on. It was easier to move loads up the ladders fast because the hands stayed free to help with the climb.

Today, the cargo boxes would be filled with pungent fish entrails.

Trin wriggled into her harness. She grabbed a box and a large scoop, pushed the scoop down into the barrel of fish guts, and slopped the stuff into the box until it was loaded. She only gagged three times before the box was full and sealed.

'Crankin', I love guts day.' She mimed another gag for Sharly.

'Flowin',' said Sharly, trying to talk without breathing until the lid on her box was sealed.

When the boxes were loaded up with rank guts, they headed up the zigzag of ladders to the top of the cliff. On the way up, Trin sensed that new signal again. It drew her attention out to sea, out behind Lighthouse Island. But every time she paused to concentrate, scanning for signs of a school of fish, or pod of whales, or maybe a boat, the feeling slipped away. There was nothing to be seen.

At the top of the cliffs the team pushed through the narrow opening in a thick, dense hedge that had been grown to give the gardens some protection from the wind and storms. Mal unhooked Trin's cargo box; Trin stretched her shoulders and returned the favour for Mal. Then she broke the seal on her box and there was a hiss as the stench escaped from the warming sludge. She tipped it into the compost vat, being careful to duck out of the way as the gross putrefying concoction splashed up.

'Okay, get those boxes cleaned up,' called one of the techs that the fishers had nicknamed Bio Bob. 'You grommets will be taking down a load of vegies to the kitchen.'

'Yay! I love scrubbing out the guts,' said Trin, miming one last gag.

'Guts is crank,' added Sharly.

'Would you rather scrub or have guts in your dinner?' asked Bio Bob.

'Scrub,' chorused the fishers. The thought of guts motivated them to scrub harder.

'Nearly done?' asked Bio Bob. Not waiting for an answer, he continued. 'While your boxes are drying, you grommets are rostered on for bug duty.'

'Pluck and plop?' asked Raz.

'Yeah, do the rounds and collect the little vegie munchers, but make sure you put them all into the vats. I don't want to waste any fertiliser.'

'Pluck and plop.' Sharly shivered. 'Drowning in the vats, what a way to go.' She always sympathised with the bugs.

Trin thought about the drowning part. She guessed that all the fishers thought about drowning sometimes, with the amount of time they spent in the water. She had a sudden vision of being under the water, way under. She gasped.

'Burley for brains.' Sharly's voice interrupted Trin's frightful vision.

'What?' said Tennan, lifting his boot to inspect a squashed bug. 'I was just performing a mercy killing.' He prized the insect off the rock and flicked it into the fertiliser vat.

'Here, Sharly.' Bio Bob handed Sharly a spraypack. 'You can follow the hunters and use the spray. It'll discourage new munchers. It's all organic, mostly chilli powder mixed with soapy water. It'll burn the bugs' mouths if they chew on a leaf, or burn their little bug butts when they sit on the plants. Either way, it'll stop the munchers eating the crops before we can.'

This hands-on approach was essential for the garden. No one at the station could bear the idea of messing with the environment any more than humans already had, so they weeded and sprayed and flung hungry little critters into the vats without complaining ... much.

Trin was glad to straighten up and stretch after her time as a weeding machine. She picked up the cargo box from where she had left it drying in the sun and sniffed it to make sure every molecule of fish guts was gone. Then she went over and loaded it up with fruit and vegetables for the kitchens.

'First one down doesn't have to rake the kelp,' called Tennan.

Trin had forgotten about cleaning up the mess left behind by yesterday's storm.

Tennan waved and headed for the gap in the hedge.

Trin fumbled to clip her loaded box onto her harness and raced after him. Mal stepped in front of her as she entered the hedge track. He slowed down as he tried to fasten his cargo box. She shuffled along behind him to help. This caused her to cop a few scratches as she pushed through the hedge, but it was worth it to speed them both up.

The kelp was always knee deep on the rock ledge after the storm. It had lain in the sun all morning, so it would be another massive stink to deal with after lunch. If she could get ahead of Tennan and down the snakes first, she would have one less stink in her day.

Mal and Trin had caught up with Tennan by the time he reached the cliff edge, and this was their chance to get ahead.

No one working up top would survive a traffic jam if a sudden storm came, so there were plenty of snakes for everyone. Tennan was fumbling with his safety knot. Trin rushed past him, grabbed a snake and clicked her descender into place. Her hands flew on the safety knot. Out of the corner of her eye, she saw Mal already heading over the top, but she would be right behind him.

She leaped out and let gravity speed her over the edge; this was her favourite part of the descent. The descender whistled on the rope as she sailed through the air for a few metres, then she planted her feet wide on the rock wall and pushed off again with all her might.

Doing this, she felt she was flying, free of the rock and the earth for a few wonderful seconds. She arced in towards the cliff, braced, and pushed off again. The descender squealed along the rope as she flew down the cliff face between each bounce off the rock wall.

There was that feeling again: a whispering signal inside her head, coming from the water. She was too curious to resist and turned to snatch a look. She felt sure there would be something to see this time. Wrong. There was still nothing there, and now she had lost concentration. She was off balance and coming into her next landing point on the cliff unbraced and at totally the wrong angle. The rock wall came at her in a flash. She didn't have time to turn and get her feet between her body and the unforgiving stone.

Smack. Her shoulder and hip hit the cliff, but she was grateful that most of the impact was absorbed by the cargo box.

The descender locked, and Trin bounced and flailed around on her line like a fish caught on a hook. She was winded and embarrassed, but unhurt. She would not be first to the bottom. She saw that Mal had won, and Tennan was doing a wild tantrum dance.

She laughed as she slid down the rest of the snake. Tennan was much better at coming second, or last, than he was at winning, and he was much more entertaining grumpy than he was gloating.

After the team spent the afternoon wrestling large clumps of stinky kelp back into the ocean, Trin logged onto the computer for her scheduled daily lessons. Meg monitored each of their study files very closely, but Trin knew she was getting excellent grades. She was doing extra science subjects because she wanted to qualify for a position studying science at Whitlam.

The added bonus of having such good study results was that it helped convince Meg that Trin was feeling well, which meant that Meg spent less time checking Trin's health.

Trin's mum had been sick and not survived whatever it was she had had. Trin had similar symptoms when she was a baby, but she had been symptom free for ages—mostly free, anyway. At least she could hide the times when she was unwell from Meg. Trin wasn't about to share every detail about every little dizzy spell or bout of nausea, and certainly not anything else that might make Meg ban her from the water.

Anyway, being in the water always made her feel better. When she swam she felt energised. All of the fishers had grown up here at the station and spent half their lives in the water. She thought maybe they'd all sprout gills one day.

Trin logged off lessons at sunset and settled herself on the ledge of the cave entrance to watch the last light of the day leak out of the sky. Between the kelp and the lessons, there was no time for swimming today, but at least she could look at the sea. She loved watching the orange-and-red glow in the sky before everything faded to a velvet-indigo that wrapped the earth and the ocean in a starry night blanket.

The water close to the rock ledge had already faded to grey in the shadow of the cliff. Further out, the last red from the setting sun was filling the sea with ruby sparks. The wind had dropped out and the sea was tranquil, the swell rising and falling like a gentle breath. The gulls and the other day birds were settling down, concerning themselves only with fluffing their feathers and tucking their heads under their wings for the night.

Trin had learned from her dad that sunset was a time to stop and reflect. He had taught her to thank the day for what it had brought her. She smiled. 'Thank you,' she whispered, thinking of the cargo box full of vegies that had saved her from breaking a rib or two.

As the last colour faded from the water, Trin heard the sound of an outboard motor approaching from around Lighthouse Island. No, the sound seemed to change direction. She scoured the darkening sea, looking for the boat but couldn't see anything. Maybe it was coming from the north, past the Funnel. Now she couldn't hear anything.

Yes, there it was again, but it seemed mixed up with petrels calling each other as they headed out for a night of hunting. The birds' calls rose up again. Maybe it was all just the birds and not a motor at all.

'Did you hear the boat?' Sharly's head appeared at the ledge and Trin jumped.

'I thought it was the night birds heading out.' Trin listened again and heard the boat, but this time the sound seemed to be fading, as though it was moving away from shore.

'It dropped someone off, see?' Sharly pointed down to where pale light from the dining hall spilled across the rock ledge.

'This is a weird time for an arrival.' Trin scanned the water. She was more interested in seeing where the boat was. She could definitely hear it pulling away, but she couldn't see any wake lines reflected in the darkening water.

She moved her focus to the water's edge. There were people gathered there in the gloom. She could see Meg, her dad and Jasper talking to two visitors. The newcomers appeared to be dressed for swimming. The light from the barely risen moon shimmered off their wetskins, making them look like dark pearl.

'Why would they be wearing wetskins now? No one goes into the water at night anymore,' Trin said.

'They're not,' said Sharly.

'Yeah, look, they're wearing skins and they're wet.'

'They look like two guys in shorts and T-shirts to me.'

Trin strained her eyes. Even with the beam of Jasper's torch lighting things up a bit, she found it hard to see details, but the visitors still looked to her like they were wet and reflecting the moon's light.

'Well, let's not just sit here staring,' Sharly said, 'I'm sure they'll be offering our visitors dinner. Let's go to the dining hall and check them out properly.'

Sharly zipped down the snake, and Trin clipped on and followed her.

In the dining hall, everyone was clustered around a table where Trin assumed the two guys were sitting. Trin thought they must be scientists, but whoever they were, she couldn't see them through the crowd. The station didn't get many visitors. Too many people from inland were scared away from the coast by the idea of the big storms.

Jasper was struggling from the kitchen with a large tray heavily loaded with bowls of fish stew, bread, and some of the fruit Trin and the others had snaked down from the gardens. Trin's dad and Meg were pushing their way through the throng to sit and eat with the mystery guests.

Curious, Trin joined the crowd around the table.

Mal, who was hovering on the edges, started relaying news as soon as she was close enough to hear it. 'They've come in from one of the island outposts. They want to do an information exchange and pick up some supplies.'

'I thought I heard them say they were looking for people to help with a new project,' Raz said.

'Sick,' said Sharly, and she did a mini happy dance.

'Maybe you should save the dancing until you know if it's true,' said Mal.

Meg caught sight of Trin and beckoned her to come closer. 'Trin, come and meet our guests from ...'

'Station ... Nakki Station,' said a breathy voice from behind the last few shoulders.

Trin stepped forward and nudged her way through the gap in the crowd to greet their guests. As the gap widened for her, she caught sight of the visitors and froze.

They were blue, shimmering. Not the blue luminescence that could be seen some nights when the algal blooms jammed up against the rocks and flared like the water was full of blue fireworks. No, these visitors were truly, liquidly blue, with wet-looking blue skin, blue, ropey hair and bare chests. She couldn't see evidence of any clothing.

Trin felt as though she had just been plunged into the ocean in winter as her breath was forced from her lungs.

The two blue heads turned and locked eyes with her, then looked at each other. The scene in front of Trin abruptly rippled and changed. All at once she saw sandy-coloured station uniforms fizz into view, topped by damp straggly hair and tanned faces.

'Did you see that, Sharls? Who are these shubees?' Trin said. She felt a huge pressure behind her eyes as the visitors stared at her. 'What's going on?' she managed to croak before she passed out.

THE BELOW

*S*he went up there again, Father. Alone. Lana's skin flashed red with spite-filled delight.

Is this true, Rilla?

Yes, Father. Rilla glared at Lana and sent her a hateful, stabbing neume.

Lana winced, but continued. *This is the third time I've seen her up there, unaccompanied, since she made her promise to you. She's been spending a lot of time close in, at the shore, and today she was watching and listening, with her ears. She was singing their songs and talking with their words. I heard her.*

I didn't want to lift my head out of the water, but I had to be sure.

Thal gave Lana a pained, questioning smile. *While you had your loyal head out of the water, did you think to offer your sister counsel or guidance?*

Lana's red paled to a sickly grey. *I wanted you to know what she'd been doing, Father. You gave her only one more chance.*

Leave us, Lana. Lana lingered. *Now!* Father's neume of displeasure boomed in Rilla's mind as it rippled through the Hall of Colours.

Lana withdrew, but only a short distance.

Thal, what's happening? Rilla's mother slipped in close beside her husband and tried to tangle their tails as she often did to help soothe him.

Thal's tails stiffened, as though they had become walker legs, and he glared at his wife.

Ula tried once more, curling her tails and letting a fin brush across her husband's darkened skin, but he remained rigid. She cast a worried look towards Rilla, who was pale with concern. Then to Lana, who glowed orange, unable to hide her gloating.

She's your sister, Lana, and you choose to shirk the duties of the promise you made, neumed Ula. *Then you deal with her in this cruel way.*

Lana became even paler and withdrew a little more.

Your youngest daughter has shamed us, Thal thundered at Ula.

Our youngest daughter is young, and not yet as wise as her father. Thal, you know how unsettling the time of choosing can be for the young.

Thal turned away from his wife and glared at Rilla. *Why must you do this thing, Rilla?*

I'm curious.

You're curious, Thal repeated, shaking his head. He looked up at the few members of the Gathering of Colours who were watching from the back of the hall.

Rilla saw them watching and tried to neume privately with her father. *But the Above is so full of colour and the walkers look so interesting. I just want to learn more about the Above.*

Thal's neumes thudded into her mind. *Enough of this foolishness, I'm sending you to the Deeps, to spend time with Pelagya in the kelp forest.* He glanced at the onlookers. *You can stay there for the remaining moon cycle until your choosing, and learn more about the Below and the history of the Abrax.*

Panic squirmed up from Rilla's stomach, bringing the threat of regurgitation. She swallowed hard. *Father, no!*

The Deeps, Thal? Ula grew pale. *Is that necessary?*

Pelagya will help our daughter appreciate the colours of the Abrax, and her rightful place in the Below. Then he turned to Rilla again. *These reckless impulses to visit the Above are dangerous. I don't know how you find anything to be curious about in that filthy world. We should all stay down here in the Below, doing what we can to repair the damage the walkers have done to Mother Ocean with their poisons.*

Rilla retightened the grip she had on her hidden thoughts. If her father found out now about the choice she had already made, she might never return from the Deeps. She gulped deeply to try and calm herself, then she chanced an appeal. *Father, perhaps the Abrax and the walkers could help each other with the healing.*

Us help the pestilent walkers? Her father darkened and lifted his fin.

Rilla braced for him to strike her, but her mother's tails flashed out and seized him. *Thal, how dare you.* Mother was black.

Ula. He bowed his head ever so slightly in a gesture only family would have recognised. *These neumes of hers … how can she think such things?* His face saddened as he turned towards Rilla. *I've neumed with Pelagya. The wise crone has offered to help you with your strange ideas.*

Rilla knew she had been naïve to think her father would ever let her choose to ascend. No wonder she had never known any Abrax who chose to take the catalyst. Were all such Abrax taken to the Deeps? She stiffened, rippling neither gill nor fin. Staring and neuming for mercy.

Her father's tails gripped her mother's tightly. *Take her now*, he ordered the guards.

Thal, no! Ula struggled to free herself from her husband's grip and go to her daughter, but Thal held her tails tightly. Ula's skin paled as she stretched out her hand towards Rilla's.

Mother! Rilla lunged forward before the guards closed in and gripped her mother's hand tightly.

Ula scowled at the approaching guards and they hesitated. *This is cruel and unnecessary*, she pleaded with Thal, but he turned his face away from them both.

Rilla blasted out a strong neume of distress, hoping Neeva was close enough to sense her. *Can I see Neeva to say farewell before I go?* Rilla implored her father, hoping to delay leaving and give her mother time to think of a way to change his mind.

What's happened? Neeva dove in, shoving between the guards and Rilla, and quickly tangled her tails with her sister's.

Rilla gushed the hurt and frustration about what Lana had done. *Father is sending me away, to the Deeps.* She and Neeva glared hatefully in Lana's direction, and she withdrew into the shadows.

Just for looking at the Above, Father? Neeva neumed in her sister's defence. *But going to the Above is a rightful part of the choosing.*

She promised not to go alone. Thal cast an eye towards the city elders, who were now gathering in the Hall of Colours.

Neeva gave Rilla a sad stare as the guards pulled them away from each other.

Thal threw his chest out proudly and put great strength in his neume. *Studying with the crone Pelagya is a privilege, Rilla. You can celebrate with your sisters when you come back for your choosing ceremony, and we'll praise you for making the right choice.*

But, Thal—

Later, Ula.

The crowd of elders were jostling, curious about the details of the incident. Rilla watched her mother put on her wifely mask for their benefit, but Ula's skin had turned a sickly blue-grey.

Father signalled, and the two guards strengthened their grip on Rilla's arms, pulling her hand free from her mother's. They guided her firmly out of the Hall of Colours and through the pearlescent thoroughfares of Lemuria. They seemed empty, but Rilla could feel the poorly concealed neumes of hidden onlookers watching from the shadows.

The Deeps.

What a privilege.

Better her than me.

Younglings were chittering about hissi-weed and witches.

Rilla's heart was clenching frantically, and the water felt too thick to gulp through her gills. Her vision darkened. She shook her head, trying to dispel the swoon. Her stomach churned upwards again, but she swallowed hard and neumed one last strained appeal to the guards. *I must get my comb and pouch from my nest before I leave.*

She could feel that the guards had blocked their minds to her neumes. They led her out through the thinning edges of the city. Whey reached a concealed cleft in the rock of the city cavern that Rilla had never noticed before, and guided her along a narrow, twisting passageway that led out to the open ocean.

She gulped at the sight of blue fading into black beyond the cavern. She struggled to pull free and turn back to the passageway, which was already fading into the folds of rock. The guards tightened their grip and turned her around. They flicked their fins in unison and Rilla jerked forward as they started down into the darkening sea.

THE ABOVE

So how are you feeling, Little Fish?'

The words her father spoke seemed to travel through thick water before reaching Trin's ears.

'I feel a bit wiped out,' she mumbled, as the straight lines of the station clinic came into focus. 'What happened?'

'You fainted, last night at dinner.' Meg's voice came through the thinning mental fog. Her smiling face was edged with concern as it hovered above Trin.

'We brought you here and checked you out,' her dad said. 'You must've overdone it with all the extra jobs yesterday.'

'I enjoyed having company for a sleepover'—Meg was starting with the doctor jokes—'but I could hear you snoring from my bunkroom.'

'Groan,' mumbled Trin.

'Mal told us you had a bit of a prang when you were coming down the snake from the gardens,' her dad said. 'Did you hit your head?'

'You should've told me about the crash,' said Meg.

'I didn't hit my head. I just hurt my hip a little, that's all.'

'Maybe you were a bit overexcited at meeting Kayn and Andy,' her father added. 'I know how quickly word spread around the grommets about them looking for candidates to apprentice to their project.'

'Who are Kayn and Andy?'

'Our visitors, remember?'

'Are those their names?'

'I know how much you want a study spot in the program here, so I thought the rumours about a chance to get on their project might've gotten the better of your nerves and—'

'And I got excited and fainted like some vapid, swooning maiden? Really?' Trin's face burned.

'Well, I thought ... you know sometimes you get sick, Fish.' Her father's face hovered above her, full of concern.

'I'm not sick. Will you two just let me be *unsick*? I'm not Mum, okay, Dad? I'm fine, so unshackle, stop worrying. It was just those new guys—' Trin stopped herself. She was definitely not going to say, *Hey Dad,*

110

Meg, did you know that just for a second I thought our visitors looked like weird blue squid people, but then they rippled and changed. No, she was already getting enough attention.

Maybe Kayn and Andy's project involved sending out mysterious brainwaves, somehow, and watching for people's reactions. And her reaction had been to pass out. *Seriously, Trin.* She let out a deep sigh and shook her head.

Maybe she really was sick. She could still feel a slight shadow of the pain remaining from last night, but she wasn't going to let that show while her dad and Meg were watching. She rolled onto her side to face the wall, letting her father know she was done with his over-protective sympathy.

'He's gone, Trin,' Meg said after a few moments. 'What were you saying about the new guys?'

'They looked strange. They surprised me.' Trin rolled back to face Meg. 'Where are they from, anyway?'

'One of the new outer stations. They said they wanted to visit a few of the larger, more established stations to get the widest selection of data possible for their project.'

'Meg, this might sound strange, but there's something about these new guys. It's just a feeling, but something's not right about them. They seemed weird, shubee, like they were faking it.'

'You didn't get much time to check if they were fake or not, Fish. You only saw them for a second before you—'

'Meg, you've seen all the vids about how bad things can be, and you know how desperate people have become since the rising. Everyone knows that we need to be cautious about things and people that don't seem right.'

'But Kayn and Andy do seem right, Trin. While I was sitting here with you last night, I spent some time tracking their credentials. I was wondering, too. I'd never heard that they'd established any new stations.'

Meg paused for a long moment. 'This new station called … um … Nakki. The search was tricky. The computer was really glitching last night, so I had to dig for hours to track down the info about it.' Meg rubbed her temples and looked like she was struggling to remember. She zoned out for a second time. 'But I finally did.'

Trin felt a throbbing behind her eyes that made her wince before it faded. Then she felt guilty, because Meg had stayed with her all night. 'You're tired, Meg. Tell me about it later.'

'No, I'm fine. I had some sleep, in between the snoring.' She smiled. 'Anyway, the search was a bit tricky, but I did find a few details about Kayn and Andy. Well, it was a bit vague, but that's not unusual with the glitches and drop-outs.' She shrugged. 'They seem to check out.' She shrugged and rubbed her temples again. 'Mostly.'

'But I saw something. I mean, I felt something, a vibe, a hunch.'

'Tell me about what you felt just before you passed out.' Meg had taken on her patronising doctor tone.

Trin shrugged a casual, no-big-deal shrug and swallowed down the rest of her observations about the visitors. 'Maybe you're right, Meg. Maybe I did hit the rock too hard.'

'How do things look for you when you're swimming, diving?'

'What's that got to do with this?'

'Tennan said something about you ... sensing the location of the fish. Is that what you think you can do?'

'I'll have that squid's brains for burley.' Trin boiled with the sense of betrayal.

'Hey, come on, it's not his fault. I was digging for information after you collapsed last night. I fired a lot of questions at them. Maybe I used a bit too much of my Meg-the-boss pressure and Tennan buckled.'

'So what, now you've found another thing to prove I'm an invalid?'

'No, Trin, but I want to make sure you're okay. There could be something causing some kind of hallucinations.'

'Are you kidding me?' Trin's head spun; she felt as though she had a net full of fish in her belly. She could have ... a tumour, some defect in her brain. 'So you think there's something wrong with my brain.'

'No, Trin, I'm sorry, no.' Meg took hold of Trin's hands. 'I didn't mean to scare you, Fish. I'm sure there'd be other signs if your brain ... I just want you to be well. You need to get checked out, anyway. You won't get a spot on a project team without a health clearance, none of us do.'

'I get it, no more doctor talk.' The fish in Trin's belly quieted, but not much. 'All right, test me. Let's see if I've got burley for brains.'

'I haven't got the scanning equipment here at the station, but that's good news.'

'In what way is there good news about needing to have a brain scan?'

'I was going to High and Dry to drop off reports and trade for some supplies. They have a scanner there at the medical centre, and the test doesn't hurt a bit and I'm sure the results will come back clear.' Meg smiled. 'You and Sharly can come for a couple of days. You haven't been there since you were little. It'll be fun for you. The Monsoon Festival will be starting. It'll be a nice break. We'll leave first thing tomorrow.'

'I don't need a break. I love being here near the sea.' The thought of spending days at High and Dry made Trin cringe, but she knew Meg would win out. 'Okay, I'll go with you. Like I have a choice, but Meg, please don't say anything thing to Dad about the scan thing. At least until there's something to say.'

Meg smiled and shrugged. 'Okay.'

'Thanks, Meg.' Trin got to her feet, wobbling slightly but hiding it. 'I'm going for breakfast, then I'll go tell Sharls and start getting ready.'

She headed out of the clinic into the dazzling morning light. She walked towards the water and stood on the edge of the rock platform, with the sea lapping gently over her feet. There were no signals today, not a mumble. The seas were getting emptier. There were far fewer fish worldwide now that the salinity levels were dropping, so there were probably no fish at all here today.

Trin was grateful for the quiet. Her eyes drifted across the sequined turquoise of the water and out to Lighthouse Island. The water in the Blender was as peaceful as she ever remembered seeing it. Staring at the island, she felt a prickle in her mind. There was no reason to go to the island, and a massive rule stated emphatically that no one could ever go across the Blender.

But the prickle remained and grew stronger, and she knew she was going there, today, now. Before she had to leave with Meg and spend days landlocked at High and Dry. If they scanned her brain and told her there was something in her head that shouldn't be there, everything would change. So she had nothing to lose except her curiosity about what was—maybe—on Lighthouse Island.

THE BELOW

Having attuned her ears so keenly so that she could listen to the distant sounds of the Above, Rilla was now overwhelmed by the rushing, gurgling noises that surrounded her. The sound of the water flowing past her ears was like a slow, wailing wind. Her arms throbbed from the guards' tight grip as they swam ceaselessly on, descending the rock slope that was being swallowed by the blackness of the ocean below.

She squirmed and tried to turn and look up to glimpse the distant sun, before it was lost from sight, but the guards held her firmly.

Still yourself, shamed youngling. The neume was oily in her mind.

I'm not shamed. I was curious and I'm not a youngling. She squirmed harder.

You're not anything right now. Your own father wants you out of Lemuria.

She faded to grey and sagged in their grip. *I want my sister.* Rilla flooded the guards' minds with the desperation and sad shock she was holding inside. *Please stop, just for a while, and let me neume to her before we're too far away.*

She felt her plaintive neume slap back at her mind as the guards blocked her again. They turned and glared at her, then gripped her harder and increased their speed, dragging her even faster into the darkness. She could find no compassion in their hearts.

The silent journey towards the Deeps had felt endless, but now the descent wasn't so steep. Her mind groped at hope-filled fantasies. *Maybe Father was just playing a cruel taunt to teach her a lesson, and soon they would circle around and head back home.* No. The descent might not have been steep any longer, but they were still heading steadily downward.

Rilla had never been so far from Lemuria before. Each time she sensed that the guards had opened their minds to her, she neumed her questions and fears. She was met with an uneasy disregard, but they couldn't hide flickers of their own apprehension. They didn't want to be going to the Deeps any more than she did. They would be returning home once she was delivered, but they still neumed wisps of fear. How terrible was this Pelagya creature? Would she ever be allowed to return?

There was another dark flash of neume from one of the guards. The strangeness of the image made Rilla shiver, but it was gone before she could understand it. Something in the Deeps truly frightened them. Their minds clamped shut.

The three swam steadily downward and the water grew darker, thicker. Rilla saw almost no creatures moving around them now, but she could feel them. They were close, hidden. When their neumes crossed her mind, they were like creeping shadows. She welcomed the sound of the sea moaning in her ears. She wished it were louder and blocked the baleful neumes coming from out of the dark from these hidden creatures.

The water was so cold now. It didn't seem like they were approaching the sanctuary that had saved the Abrax back in the time of the Great Darkening. The history neumes told that warm water from vents in the Deeps stopped the sea in this region from becoming deathly cold, as it had in so many other places, but the water was still numbingly cold. The relatively warm water had saved the Abrax, and they had gained courage from each other by staying together.

Rilla had no one but the guards, and soon she would be left alone with Pelagya. What would the old crone do to her? She had never felt so alone, even when she spent time in the Above with all its strangeness. A heavy dread welled up inside her. Her tails stiffened like driftwood.

The guards ignored her distress and swam steadily on, pulling her deeper and deeper. The water felt thick now, and frigid, chilling her to the bone. She tried to block the painful coldness by imagining herself sitting on the warm rocks so very far above, watching Marcus and the other walkers as they laughed and talked in the sunshine. Then she imagined floating in the warm water, looking up at the birds soaring in the endless blue sky.

A glow coming up from somewhere below brought her out of her thoughts with a shudder. The darkness was fading; she dreaded to think what she would see.

The pale red light grew in intensity as they glided down into a sloping rock valley. Silhouetted against the glow, Rilla saw a dark kelp forest swaying in the current. The broad, ponderous blades of kelp stretched up, the black snarl rippling in unison.

Rilla noticed other plants at the edges of the kelp forest. They were thinner, feeble. They didn't ripple in the current, but instead moved unnaturally against the rhythm of the ocean's flow, writhing, struggling. Rilla felt a shadowy half-formed neume coming from them. She shivered and clenched her gills shut.

The guards bristled as they reached the sparse sloping edges of the kelp forest. Feeling their unease, Rilla tried to appeal to them once again.

I'm frightened, she neumed. *Please take me home.*

The guards only glanced at her and then looked past her, towards each other.

Frightened is the right thing to be, youngling, one of the guards neumed.

They glowed orange, gloating and amused. She felt their minds close with such force that she winced.

A wave of panicky heat flashed through her body. The ugly brown-black-red of the Deeps blurred around her as her mind twisted at the horror of the thought that had entered her mind. Her stomach clenched and she tasted hot sourness in her mouth. She swallowed hard.

I might never see the Above again.

A neume burst through her panic. *Not far now.*

The guards had turned to face the kelp forest, and now they continued cautiously up to the edge. They hesitated before threading their way through the beginnings of the tangle. Around them, the thinner, smaller plants writhed like eels. Was it reaching for them? But how could it be? Rilla shuddered each time the plants swayed close to her.

Near the edge of the forest of kelp, the temperature of the water was warmer. Up ahead, above the billowing darkness of the forest, the red glow grew in intensity. Not the skin red the Abrax showed during debate and argument, but an alive red that burst up from time to time, pushing into the dark sea above the forest.

As Rilla watched, the fingers of red flickered down again, and then there was an eruption of orange, followed by sparks of brightness like sunlight on water. When the reds and oranges flared, she could see the heated water twisting and rising, like angry eels, into the vast cold darkness above. The warming water was easier to swim through, but the currents twisted and curled around each other.

As the forest of kelp towered up in front them, the younger of the guards began swimming haltingly. *Is it much further?* he neumed.

We're entering Pelagya's realm now, neumed the older guard.

The young guard tightened his grip on Rilla's arm and stared around nervously. A yellowy paleness of fear crept across his skin. Rilla shared his emotion and pallor.

I really believed the witch was just a part of the old myths, neumed the young guard.

Pelagya is very real, answered the older guard. *And she's capable of many things.*

Though the water was warm, Rilla shivered, remembering the whispered stories of what Pelagya could do. Such stories had travelled on the neumes, causing paleness in many younglings throughout Lemuria. The younglings often asked how true the tales were, but the adults never answered. So the younglings, including Rilla, had relegated Pelagya to the world of half-truths, to be forgotten with time.

Now the sea-witch had suddenly leapt out of the long-dismissed tales and become real, mysterious and frightening. Rilla had been banished to this place by her father, to be taught a lesson before her choosing ceremony, but she had already made her decision. How would Pelagya respond when she discovered this?

How well can I block the crone from my mind? How will she punish me when she discovers my truth? Rilla redoubled her efforts to hide her secret deep in her mind.

They swam on, pushing through the slick tangled blackness of the kelp forest. Ahead, Rilla glimpsed bright stripes of orange and red glowing through the dense forest. The young guard shifted from view. He still held Rilla's arm, though less firmly than before, and he had dropped back as if hiding behind her to shield himself from the heat—and the witch. The older guard pulled her through the heavy blackness, while the younger nudged her in the back to move her forward. With each tug and shove, the guards moved Rilla closer to this otherworldly place where water could burn.

The kelp grew even more densely here, and Rilla felt the velvety slime of the kelp slide along her skin. Now both guards had moved behind her, and the kelp almost wrapped itself around her. She felt a smothering pressure as the guards pushed her forward. The slick pelt of the kelp slithered across her face. She twisted, trying to move away from each frond, only to be slapped and swathed by the next.

The dark snarls of kelp finally parted and her vision filled with a blinding radiance. She blinked until the pain eased in her eyes and her vision cleared. The guards had stopped shoving. It appeared she had arrived at her destination.

Enjoy your lessons, neumed the older guard.

When will you come back for me?

That'll be up to Pelagya.

There was a final shove and the guards' hands released her. She turned and saw them disappear back through the forest. She tried to follow, but, with a ripple, the kelp closed tightly, forming a dark wall.

She was alone in the sea-witch's realm.

THE ABOVE

No one noticed Trin walk to the end of the peninsula. She looked back along the curve of the rock shelf. The cliff face glowed in the early sunshine. Except for the lab and Meg's clinic, the shutters on the caves remained closed, dark spots on the rock wall. Sharly had left the shutters open, by habit, but Trin always left them open to hear the sea at night.

Trin's eyes drifted back across the glinting water. Everything was still. She turned to face the island. Hanging her toes over the edge, she watched the water churning for a long while. With no wind yet, the conditions were exceptionally calm in the Blender.

She heard voices behind her. Looking over her shoulder, she saw the fishers clambering up the ladders with those two weird guys. Everyone was out to impress them and get placement on their project, but Trin needed to spend time with her thoughts, to try and make sense of what was happening inside her head.

Could she really have something wrong with her brain? Is that what was causing her to believe she was communicating with the fish? Did she have some neurological glitch that made her see and hear things? Would the glitch be serious enough to kill her? She would know soon enough.

Pacing back and forth, she judged the narrowest point of the Blender. Then she balked. She was about to do the one thing that no one at Whitlam ever did, and she was going to do it alone.

This is the Blender. What am I doing? I might not need to worry about my brain.

The whispering, prickling sensation frothed into her mind again, and she felt overwhelmed by a sense of confidence, reassurance that she would make the crossing safely.

The momentum of her dive pushed her two-thirds of the way across the choppy water of the channel. She surfaced and the waves slapped her in the face. She coughed out the water and started swimming hard. Even though it was a calm day, the current was still running fiercely. She was immediately grabbed by the permanent

125

rip that ran through the Blender and dragged quickly to the south. The water twisted widely as it moved through the deeper places in the channel, and she was sucked down and held under as the water tumbled down on top of her. She swam hard to escape the twisting water spirals, clawing up to gasp a breath before she was pulled along and down again.

Her muscles burned as she strained to keep her head above the surface. She searched for a place between the jutting rocks and hoped she could reach it.

When she had finally fought her way across to the island, she was well around the southern side and the peninsula blocked the sight of her from anyone at the station who might happen to look her way. She scrambled up onto the rough honeycomb of rock at the island, panting but proud.

Lighthouse Island was jagged and windswept. A few relentless bushes clawed their roots deep into the cracks in the rock. Their branches pointed stiffly in the direction the wind had been blowing them since they were seedlings. Even the lighthouse looked as though it was leaning slightly, losing its battle with the wind and storm-driven waves.

The wind was lifting as the sun rose higher in the sky, and the breeze moaned around the lighthouse tower. Trin stood listening. Even with the eerie sounds, she felt soothed by this place.

The wind gusted and the door at the base of the lighthouse squeaked rhythmically on its salt-corroded hinges. Trin stepped closer, trying to see inside. The rusty hinges protested as she pushed against the weathered door and stepped into the circular stone room.

Each step Trin took stirred up plumes of dust from the floor. Four beams of light came through a row of small windows in the curved wall and formed a glowing crisscross pattern in the drifting dust. Crisping curls of white paint dangled from the weathered woodwork and furniture, but apart from the decay the place was tidier than she had expected. She thought the floor should have been carpeted with crusty piles of bird droppings. If she were a bird, she would choose to shelter here, especially when the storms came.

There was that whisper again, but it was much clearer now. Was it louder? Her heart skipped and she turned quickly to look at the door, expecting to see someone there.

'Just the wind.' Her voice sounded too loud as it bounced off the curved walls.

The wind was puffing in through a crack in one of the windows, ruffling a shred of fabric hanging at its edge. She stepped over to the window and pushed the rag aside. She thought for a moment she had glimpsed someone outside, but no, it was just a scraggy tree blown by the wind. Maybe there *was* something wrong inside her head.

She walked around the curving wall, trailing her fingers along the painted stone until she reached the stairs. They curled up around the wall of the tower and disappeared into the next level. Trin rattled the wooden banister railing to see how solid the stairs were, then she ventured up a few steps and jumped up and down. Her curiosity won out against her sense of caution. Too late to start being cautious now, she reasoned. She'd already broken the biggest station rule by coming here. And she might have something monstrous growing inside her head. No time to cut back now.

Trin climbed the spiral stairs slowly, stamping her feet to test each step as she went. Each small window along the way offered a different postcard view of her life at the station: lab, funnel, caves, gardens.

She pushed back the decaying hatch and came out on the circular ledge at the top of the lighthouse. The glass lens in the lamp was shattered, and the light mechanism inside was pimpled with rust and collapsing in on itself.

Trin risked a quick glance across the water to the station, then moved out of sight and eased herself down onto the splintering ledge. The feeling of someone watching her persisted, but she pushed it aside. She also pushed away the guilt for sneaking over to the island.

I never get to be really alone, she thought. This is crankin'. She smiled and swung her legs backward and forward through the nothingness at the top of the tower.

Now that she was truly alone and didn't have to worry about other people's questions, she concentrated on opening her mind to whatever sensations she might feel. The prickling, urgent feeling had faded when she crossed the Blender. She breathed deeply, calmly, and became aware of a quiet whispering that seemed to be made up of emotions and ... colours. It couldn't be fish because she was out of contact with the water. It felt as though her own thoughts were somehow mixing with someone else's and she was part of both at once. Whatever it was, it was nothing like the fishes' chittering.

Was it connected to what had happened last night? She wasn't ever going to let Meg know, but she was petrified about what might be growing inside her head. She was glad that she could have the scan and know for sure she was okay. I have to be okay, she told herself.

All at once there was a wave of ... something, a sense of wellness, of being ... appropriate? Suited? Befitting? It wasn't really words, more like pictures ... an amalgam of ideas and images. Her mind filled with confidence, reassurance that she was fine, that she was healthy and normal. Part of her mind knew that she should be feeling frightened by sensing this new signal, but she just wasn't.

I guess I'm better at positive thinking than I realised, she thought. The squirming fish feeling had returned to her belly. Knowing it wouldn't help if she freaked out, she took another deep breath. She would learn the answer soon enough.

The signal strengthened, and the feeling that the scans would show she was well persisted and filled her mind. Trin swung her feet in the high air again and concentrated on enjoying the view she had broken the biggest station rule for.

The whispering faded, and in the quiet void Trin was suddenly frightened to be on the island, alone. The feeling that she was being watched grew stronger again. She quickly, and much less cautiously, descended the curved stairs of the tower. Pushing through the door, she sprinted across the rocks, hoping she had the strength to survive the swim back. She ran at the water and dived in, hoping the momentum would help.

The rip was stronger now, but to her relief the current ripped her through the channel, clear of the island and the rocks. She was spun by the swirls of current and spat out the southern side of the peninsula. With barely any strength left, she swam slowly across the rip and pulled herself up onto the warm rock, shaking and shivering.

As she walked back around to the station, she stared across the churning water towards the lighthouse. The rag in the broken window fluttered, and for a moment she was convinced she had seen a face.

The Below

§preading out in front of her was a circular clearing enclosed by a towering black wall of kelp. Rilla could see the source of the red warmth she had glimpsed on her way through the forest. Seeing this for herself, she could easily understand why the Abrax believed and neumed that the sea burned down here in the Deeps.

Within the circle of high black kelp was a smaller ring of rock pillars that spewed out a burning red liquid that boiled with spitting, angry sparks. Where this eruption of red met the water, there was a hissing bubbling frenzy that created a miniature storm of eddies.

Currents of hot water twisted into the surrounding colder water, and then swirled out above the forest and into the dark valley beyond.

Rilla was mesmerised at the sight of the bubbling pillars. Memories of lessons about the vents in the Deeps flashed into her mind, and for a moment her fascination at seeing this place pushed aside her fears. She understood now why the kelp was able to grow so thickly away from the light. The heat and nutrients coming from the vents caused this precocious growth, but there was something else about the thick forest surrounding this place that was strange.

She saw more of the misshapen plants that moved unnaturally. They should be slanting and undulating in the direction of the hot current's flow, but they seemed to be struggling against the force of the heated eddies.

Squinting past the glare of the glowing pillars to the other side of the circle, Rilla could see a dark figure silhouetted by the fire from a vent. This must be Pelagya.

Rilla edged around the circle, trying to keep a distance between herself and the witch. She felt a prickle in her mind, and that she was being drawn toward the witch, but she resisted, choosing to circle around to her slowly and take in as much of her strange new surroundings as she could.

Her eyes trailed from the black shape of the sea-witch to a tall tapering structure that looked like it had been created out of shining black coral. It was shaped similarly to the Hall of Colours, but was much smaller. Why would Pelagya need a gathering place? There were no Abrax here for her to gather with.

No, Rilla corrected herself, *I'm here for my lessons.* But how many others had been sent here before her? And why had none of them ever shared their experiences when they returned?

Something brushed past Rilla's arm. A stunted frond of the strange weed floated up and wrapped around her, encircling her gird. She turned and reached out to untangle herself. As she grasped the frond, two eyes blinked opened on the dark surface.

Help.

She gulped and pushed the blinking face away. All around her, spindly ribbons of weed-creatures swayed up and out of the shadows. Their impossible eyes were blinking open and staring at her.

Help. The faint neume echoed from the writhing half-creatures. *Help—please.*

Rilla's heart cavorted as though it had forgotten how to beat. Bile rose in her throat. She tried again to push the slick blackness of the staring weed away, but her hands slipped across its surface.

Let me go—let me go. Her neumes were frantic as she struggled, striking out at the flattened black faces.

They flinched away but returned.

Help—please.

133

She saw flashes of colour flick across the black skin of the stunted hissi-weed. First a dirty orange, then green, and grey, and quickly its skin returned to black. The eyes stared at her, still pleading, and then the neumes faded until all that remained was sorrow.

Desist! Release her!

The contorting weed-creatures disentangled themselves from Rilla and stood up rigidly at the power of the witch's neume. Then the eyes closed and each of the spindly fronds withdrew back into the swaying black wall.

While Rilla had been struggling with the hissi-weed, Pelagya had moved closer. When Rilla refocused her attention, she was startled at how close the crone now was. Rilla stiffened at the imposing presence and gulped, trying to calm herself.

You're safe, was all the witch neumed as she drifted on the current.

Rilla could only stare. Pelagya was clearly Abrax, but she was bulbous and dark, dull, and lacking in the pearlescent glint of the skin that every other grown Abrax possessed. The witch's cirrus was very long. The dark tendrils that grew from her head drifted and swirled on the current, reaching almost to the edge of the clearing. The wispy, tapering ends stretched towards the surrounding kelp, touching it lightly. The cirrus that fringed her gird formed a thick black skirt that hid her tails and fins. She looked to Rilla like an anemone that had somehow been freed from the rock and was able to move itself about.

Rilla froze in place. She looked around the clearing to see how she might escape. The forest was a black wall in all directions.

Up. She lifted her face towards the Above. *I could go straight up.* As she neumed this, she felt a thin wisp of hissi-weed coil around each of her tails and gripped them lightly.

Please stop thinking of me as a witch, neumed Pelagya, as she glided closer again. She gestured towards the hissi-weed, which loosened its grip on Rilla's tails and moved away. *I'm only the caretaker of the catalyst, nothing more.* Flickers of weariness and sorrow accompanied Pelagya's neume.

Pushing aside her fear, Rilla tried to summon deference for this elder. *Respectful greetings, wise Pelagya,* she neumed, sending waves of humble blue along her trembling body.

Your formality is not necessary here. Nor is your fear.

But the weed, and—

Be calm. The hissi-weed must obey my command, just as I must obey Thal's bidding. Your father hasn't sent you into danger. I'll simply do what has asked of me, and neume with you about the Abrax and the histories before your choosing.

He sent me here to stop me visiting the Above.

Spending time in the Above is your right as part of the choosing time, but your father is concerned that you don't understand your choices or their consequences clearly.

You mean I don't see the choice the way he wants me to. Rilla braced for Pelagya's reaction to her criticism of her father.

It's not my place to judge Thal's rules, just to illuminate your thinking. To help you see things as they truly are.

As they truly are? Or as Thal and the Gathering of Colours think they are?

I was asked that I share my wisdom with you, to help you make your truest decision.

Rilla jittered with swelling panic. Her heart thumped and her vision darkened around the edges. *There are neumes about you, stories about how you influence Abrax.*

A flash of green rippled through Pelagya's cirrus. *Calm yourself, young Rilla, you're not here so I can harm you.*

But those creatures ... Rilla looked back at the place where the eyes had appeared.

They hardly have the minds to attack you. They're here for something else entirely, but that's a tale for later. For a moment, Pelagya's skin dappled with a pale sadness. *And as for the legends of me, my only exceptionality is that I'm the next in a lineage of females who can trace their generations back to the time of the Great Darkening. When the first of us created the catalyst, she also created what was needed for the Abrax to have a choice—either stay below or ascend. In doing that, she removed all choice for herself, and her daughter, and all her daughters' daughters, including me. Because the females of my lineage created the catalyst, we each must take our turn to wait alone in the Deeps, guarding it, and when the time comes, pass on the guardianship and the knowledge of its creation to the next daughter.*

Rilla suddenly felt sorry for this formidable stranger, and her skin flared a deep green of disquiet at Pelagya's plight. *No one has chosen to ascend for many generations. You don't need to remain; you could leave here and return to Lemuria.*

Many thanks for your concern, Rilla, but this is the way it is. It's been so since the Great Choosing long ago, and it will remain so as long as Thal and the Gathering of Colours command it.

You could leave. We all have the right to choose. We're Abrax.

It'll never be that simple for me, or my offspring. We're obliged to be the custodians of the catalyst because it was us who created it.

But there are no restraints holding you here. Choose. Leave this place, if that's what you want. Why haven't you left already?

Pelagya stiffened, and for a long moment she was motionless, right to the ends of each flowing cirrus. *Like the tale of the mindless hissi-weed that frightened you, the tale of what holds me here is a story for later.*

THE ABOVE

The truck's engine hummed quietly. Trin looked up as the truck hit the first of many ruts in the sandy access road heading west. She turned to watch through the rear window as the gardens and the sea beyond shrank into the distance.

West, away from the sea. The thought of being so far from the sea made Trin shudder. She knew most of the population saw things differently from her. They were all happy to be inland and a safe distance away from the crazy storm surges. Away from the inundated cities and swallowed coastal towns that were now home for fish instead of people, although some people went back, curious to see the old world for themselves. Some of the flooded places had even become heritage-listed areas. Dive sites that people could pay to visit. When the conditions were safe enough, divers looking for knowledge or adventure could explore the sunken cities with a guide.

Rolling the window down, Trin took a deep breath. She could no longer smell any trace of salt in the air. She was missing the sea already. But if she couldn't be in the water, she could at least talk about it.

'Hey, Meg, have you ever done a Sydney dive?'

'Once, back when I was studying. It was amazing, but strange. At first, I just stood there and started out across the Sydney basin, looking at the tops of the old skyscrapers jutting out of the water. The rooftops had been turned into rookeries by the huge flocks of seabirds. They looked like clouds circling the buildings and diving for food.

'Once we were under the water, we glided through the empty streets. There were no people, of course, and hardly any fish. The walls of the buildings were furry with anemones. Seaweed grew out of the cracks in the old roadways, and barnacles had encrusted old signs and streetlights. Sometimes I'd get spooked by a shirt or plastic bag drifting past my face. It was all so ghostly. Then I started noticing all the other human stuff drifting on the currents and tangling around the sea life. It made me so mad to be reminded of all the stupid things people did to cause the damage. Seeing Old Sydney helped me decide about working at the stations. It was so important to focus on the future and healing.'

'Did you get to see—' Trin tried asking another question about Old Sydney, but Meg was spinning up into one of her enviro-rants.

'For decades everyone chose to ignore the warming and the changes in the weather, or at least to deny any responsibility for causing it. They spent so much money trying to prove the science wrong instead of working on new ways of doing things. Meanwhile, down in Antarctica, the warming water seeping under the ice shelf loosened the ground ice. The ice caps melted and slipped towards the coast, then millions of years' worth of fresh water dropped into the sea.'

'Like a drink filled to the top,' Trin interrupted, smiling at Meg in the rear-vision mirror. 'When you drop a chunk of ice in a glass of water, the liquid spills over the edge.'

'Sorry,' said Meg. 'I know you've heard it all before, but …'

'But,' Sharly said, smiling at Trin. They both knew how passionate Meg was. 'All that melting ice was a big deal. The fresh water caused the sea to be less salty, so species were dying … still are.'

'And that's why we do what we do at Whitlam.' Trin grinned at Meg again. 'We hang out at the new coast to help save all the little fishies.'

'Thanks, girls, sorry about the rant.' Meg smiled back.

'Funny, isn't it,' said Sharly, looking out the window at the stark, dusty landscape. 'There's so much more water since the melt, but none of it seems to be rain, not inland, anyway.'

'Why would anyone want to live out here in the desert?' said Trin.

'They feel safe here,' said Meg.

'If I had to live inland, I'd live at Murray Sea,' said Trin. 'At least it's green out there.'

'It doesn't rain much out at Murray, either,' said Meg. 'If it wasn't for the de-sal filters they'd struggle to grow the food they do.'

'I read that they used to grow almost all our food in the Murray before it flooded,' said Trin.

'They did,' said Sharly. 'When I was little, my grandfather talked about living out there when he was a kid. By the time he was in high school, the encroachment of the water had caused massive loss of farmland. He said he remembered when he could buy a Packham pear for only five dollars, then it was ten, then twenty. Then people started stealing fruit and damaging the trees. After a while they declared nearly all fruit species to be national treasures, and they were only grown in high-security stations.'

'At least at Murray they have the seawater to desalinate, like we have at the station,' Meg said. 'All of the sojourn settlements are in mostly arid areas. They don't call Sojourn Four High and Dry for no reason. All the settlement towns rely totally on collecting rainwater in the monsoon.

141

Then they still have to reclaim every drop they can from waste processing when they convert it to fertiliser.'

'So they have the compost vats, too.' Sharly pulled a face. 'Gross.'

'Waste is a luxury these days,' said Meg over her shoulder.

'Their vegies couldn't possibly taste as good as ours at Whitlam,' said Trin.

'Why not?' Sharly asked.

'They don't have fish guts to add to the mix.'

'Cut back, Trin. I need to think of the vegies as all clean and ...'

'And what, not peppered with poop particles?' Meg smiled into the mirror.

'Yuck!'

'Or garnished with guts?

'Enough! Let me wallow in denial and skip over the grosser details.' Sharly shuddered.

Trin laughed until she snorted. Maybe it wouldn't be that bad to do a road trip. It would be good to be away from the possibility of running into the creepy shape-shifting Kayn and Andy.

Maybe the hunches she had while she was at Lighthouse Island had been totally the real deal. She hadn't had any of those weird feelings or signals, or whatever they were, since they'd left Whitlam Station. Maybe that meant the scan would show everything was okay with her brain.

THE BELOW

The days of the moon cycle passed, not that the moon could be seen so far down in the Deeps, only sensed with the movement of the tides. Pelagya did tell Rilla many stories. If they were intended to be lessons to help Rilla's choosing, she decided they must have been concealed deep within the tales because none of them were anything like the lessons she had known as a youngling.

Though Pelagya had many chances to, she had not yet told the stories she had promised when Rilla had first questioned her about life in the Deeps, or challenged her about staying a prisoner of the Gathering of Colours.

Pelagya answered some of Rilla's questions, but almost always when she started a tale, the story would wriggle like an eel and end up somewhere else entirely before she had divulged any of her secrets.

The time Rilla had spent with Pelagya allowed her to see past the crone's haunting exterior, which had seemed so frightening when she first arrived in the Deeps. During their time together, Pelagya had shown Rilla true kindness and concern. She was Abrax, even if the fates had somehow imprisoned her in the Deeps, and the Deeps had made their changes on her appearance.

It was hard to measure time passing so far away from the sun, but Pelagya felt the tides.

Your banishment will be over soon, Rilla. Soon the guards will come and take you back to Lemuria so you can make the statement of your choosing.

Rilla stiffened. *When will they come?*

Soon enough. Pelagya gave a concerned smile. *Do you know your decision?*

Rilla held her muscles tightly to stop herself from jittering. She had made her choice long ago, and she wanted to tell Pelagya and ask about the catalyst. Would Pelagya go straight to her father and let him know? Would he allow her to ascend?

I want to know about the catalyst. Rilla's skin faded to grey.

Finally. I've been waiting for these questions. Pelagya smiled.

So I'm not to be punished for my curiosity? You won't tell Father?

I'm sure he didn't want you to ask such questions, but he's never forbidden me to share what I know with you.

Rilla skin glowed orange. She swam close to Pelagya and gripped her dark old hands. *Tell me everything.*

What are your questions?

What happens? How does it work? Does it really work?

I'll answer what I can. Pelagya looked deep into Rilla's eyes for a long moment, then the ideas trickled into Rilla's mind.

The catalyst is very bitter. When it's swallowed, it burns as it passes the mouth and the throat. It's believed that the same such burning sensations accompany the transformation—

Why don't you know for sure?

Once an Abrax chooses to take the catalyst and ascend, that's what they do immediately. The Gathering of Colours deemed that they never return to Lemuria, and none have been seen even trying to return. Because of this, we can only speculate about the transformation, except for what's held in the ancient neume records.

Pelagya stared off into the dark forest. Rilla felt the wispy edges of a secret thought before it was pulled back and hidden again.

Many creatures have moved from living in the ocean to living on the land. The fact that we Abrax can breathe air once we're grown shows that we're on the same path to evolve as these other creatures.

So we're supposed to live on the land. Rilla felt her heart spasm to know this truth.

One day, but the change would be very slow. The catalyst has constituents that cause these adaptations to happen far more quickly, almost instantly.

So the Abrax who wanted the catalyst believed that moving up to live in the Above would save them?

That's what they believed. They appealed to the Gathering of Colours, who conceded to a vote, and it was agreed that all Abrax could choose. The Gathering deemed that the catalyst could be contrived and the Great Choosing occurred.

The catalyst works, neumed Rilla. *Those who first chose moved successfully to live on the land, and they thrived for all of those generations. I've seen them, in the Above. How does the catalyst make the change happen?*

I cannot show you how.

Why not? Rilla challenged.

Knowing how the catalyst works would make you a prisoner like me, and I wouldn't wish that curse on anyone. Pelagya stiffened and stared past Rilla towards the mass of hissi-weed.

I'm sorry, Pelagya. I meant no disrespect, Rilla neumed with courtly formality and glowed a humble blue.

Pelagya continued with her answers, but her neume was now formal and grave. *The bitter potion is swallowed and the Abrax ascends to the Above. Its contrivance is such that it changes the Abrax form. The fins shrink and the cirrus of the gird is shed.* Pelagya softened and floated closer, touching the shirt of cirrus that writhed at Rilla's hips. Then she smoothed Rilla's head cirrus. Pushing it back from her face, she smiled. *The head cirrus falls away also.*

Rilla greyed with distress. *But I've seen the walkers and they don't have bare heads.*

Then something takes the place of the cirrus. I don't have more to share. From all we know and have seen when we've visited the Above, we believe that once the catalyst is consumed and the changing Abrax reach the Above, they're changed forever and belong there in that world.

And that's all you know?

There's something else. The neumes remain. In the histories, there are recollections that some Abrax claimed to have felt faint neumes from the changed. These distant neumes encouraged still more Abrax to choose to ascend.

I've felt these neumes, Rilla blurted. *They come from the walkers who live there now, even after all these generations.* She squeezed her neumes tightly, fearing she'd shared too much.

So that was why Thal was so angry with you for going to the Above alone. In the quiet, we can sometimes hear them, and hearing them reminds us we're not so different from each other.

He knows this?

Pelagya nodded.

Rilla let her guarded thoughts slip for a moment. *They're like us. Their neumes have shown me that.*

Pelagya stared at her. *There it is.*

Rilla squeezed her mind closed, but it was too late.

Your decision has been made, young Rilla. You've decided to ascend. Pelagya smiled, but her cirrus rippled with a yellow-grey sadness.

Rilla nodded. *I've made my choice. I will ascend.*

It's the gravest decision you will make. Once you change, you'll be alone and—

I won't be alone. Up where the shallows meet the shore, I've watched the walkers. I've shared their neumes and learnt their air-words. They want to heal Mother Ocean as much as we do, and I want to share the Abrax knowledge and help them with the healing.

That's noble reasoning, and I've felt wisps of your decision many times since you arrived.

So you'll help me? Will the catalyst work on me?

The catalyst will make changes, nothing is surer. There was a dark flicker from Pelagya's mind, then it vanished.

Do I have to go back to Lemuria and declare my decision?

That depends on whether you take the catalyst before Thal's guards return.

I could truly take it now? Rilla's excitement pushed away any concern. *Thank you.* She glowed pink. *You've offered me so much wisdom and kindness.*

It's been good to have someone to share my knowledge and stories with.

But you've never shared the tales you promised me on my first day. The tales you said were for later.

Pelagya bristled. *They're not important things for you to know.*

Then why don't you go back to Lemuria once I've ascended?

I cannot.

Tell me why you won't leave this place.

Pelagya sunk down to the warm sand and coiled her cirrus in close to her body, as though she was shielding herself from something. She began her tale. *The Gathering of Colours ensures the mothers of my line will continue to guard the catalyst as a punishment for the first of us who dared to create it.* Flecks of angry red rippled along her coiled cirrus, and Rilla felt a wave of pain within the neume.

Punishment! Rilla twined a tail around one of Pelagya's to try and soothe her.

Pelagya accepted the twining and continued. *As a youngling, I believed I was an orphan and I was raised in the grace of the Gathering of Colours. After my choosing I fell in love. We were joined and had a daughter, Pontia. Soon after she was born, I discovered that I wasn't an orphan, as I'd believed. My mother was alive and in the Deeps. I was told of my mother's fate—to be the guardian of the secrets of the catalyst. Then I was told it was my turn to share in that fate.*

Pelagya quaked and pulled Rilla's tail closer. *My daughter was plucked from my arms and lived her life thinking she was an orphan as I had. Her father and I were brought here. Only then did I begin to realise the full horror of our fate. I met my mother, who had been a prisoner of this place all my life. Loneliness and desolation had made her wither until she was thin and wretched. I watched my mother die and then I had to take her place.*

Pelagya's bundled cirrus tightened into a dark knot, and sadness flooded Rilla's mind.

Before my mother died, Pelagya continued, *she showed me my father, and then I fully understood my own wretched fate.* She turned to look at the spindly dark ribbons of weed that twitched and blinked at the edge of the kelp forest.

Rilla followed her sad gaze. The eyes in the weed stared back intently at her.

Pelagya pointed to one of the larger blinking weed-creatures. *My love is over there, and behind him you can see my father and my grandfather—sorrow.*

Those things were Abrax? Rilla felt hot bile rush up into her mouth. She swallowed hard. *But how? Why?*

To punish me for my ancestors making the choosing possible. To hold me here. My love can never leave and I couldn't bear to leave him alone.

You could go to Lemuria, get your daughter and help her escape.

You've seen that I have no colours, only black. They took my colours from me. If I leave and return to Lemuria, I would be seen, and before I could even try to explain this all to my daughter, I would be discovered and she wouldn't even have the brief happiness of love before learning her fate. One day I'll wither, and she will share my fate, but for now she has a happy life. Maybe if I can convince the right guard, I'll be able to send a potion to stop her having a female youngling.

Rage boiled in Rilla like lava. She entwined her cirrus with Pelagya's, trying to share some of the flood of anguish that came with this tragic neume.

Father would have me believe that the walkers are the most terrible creatures because of the damage they've done, but at least they're trying to make reparation. The Abrax have done this to you and your family, for generations, and they have no intention of stopping. She stared towards the Above. *I wish to ascend now.*

Consider carefully, Rilla, Pelagya neumed with strong concern. *Once there was an agent to reverse the catalyst, but the Gathering of Colours claim it was lost. If you take the catalyst, whatever happens cannot un-happen.*

What will you tell the guards?

I'll fill their minds with a neume that they'll believe to be real. I'll convince them that sharks attacked them when they were returning with you to Lemuria. Your family will mourn your tragic loss to the belly of a shark.

How can you do that?

I've practised endlessly so that one day I might help my daughter. My neume is powerful, convincing. They can't search the innards of every shark any more than they could search for you in the Above.

THE ABOVE

On the side of the road there was an ornate signpost made from a collection of repurposed bicycle parts. It held a colourful sign that read STAY HIGH & DRY IN HIGH AND DRY. A few metres further on was a second, faded but more official looking, sign SOJOURN FOUR: CITY SETTLEMENT—EVERYONE IS WELCOME HERE.

What they saw up ahead could hardly be considered a city, not compared to the way cities used to look in the history files, anyway. It was still mostly a sprawling settlement, with random buildings spread across a hastily planned streetscape.

Sojourn Four was one of a ring of new settlement cities built around the country on sites that were elevated enough to be considered safe from inundation. Scientists had used the prediction models to plot the new, safe city sites inland, and the people, when they accepted that things would not get better any time soon, had moved their lives and families inland, away from the coast. The plan was that people would migrate to the settlements, and these new citizens would put their mark on the new cities, planning, building and naming their new homes.

'Looks like we have perfect timing,' said Meg, pointing out the truck window.

Across the fields, full of stunted plants and freshly ploughed rows, the first dark clouds of the wet season were rolling in.

'Rain used to come all year round before everything warmed up,' said Meg, seeing another chance to squeeze in a science–history lesson while she had a captive audience. 'Now that the monsoon zone has widened, the rain arrives in one season, and it has to be collected and stored to irrigate the food crops and quench people's thirsts for the rest of the year. People know how vital this rain is, so monsoon season is a time of festivals and reverence to the inhabitants of High and Dry.'

'I guess rain would be a big deal if it only rained one month of the year,' said Sharly.

'Sure is, and we've got our buckets. Are you ready to party?' Meg asked.

'So we party in the buckets?' Trin laughed.

'No. The custom of the Monsoon Festival grew with the city. The refugees come from everywhere, with many religions and cultures, but the thing that unifies them all is having survived the weather so far and needing to survive the new weather patterns from now on.'

'And the buckets?' asked Sharly.

'They're a symbol of everyone's willingness to work together and do what they can to manage the harshness of the new environment. Catching water in the buckets during the festival is a symbol of their commitment to making the harvest and their new life here successful.'

'Sounds like the worst party ever,' scoffed Trin.

'If we're willing to trade food away from these people, then it's only good manners to respect their traditions, and trust me, you'll enjoy it.'

Trin watched the city grow through the windscreen. The rolling line of clouds seemed to be hovering, holding its distance, as they drove on through the dusty fields and into town.

Meg pulled the truck to a stop outside a semi-permanent-looking building with a sign that read OFFICE OF THE ENVIRONMENT. 'This is us,' she said. 'They have staff accommodation out the back. We'll stay here while we're in town.'

They all climbed out of the truck and stretched.

'So what's to do in High and Dry?' asked Trin.

'I'd recommend eating.' Meg dug into her pocket and passed over a heavy handful of coins. 'You'll get food here that you wouldn't get at home, a feast from around the world ... delicious. And check out the breeding station at the aquarium. That's where the tank of viable specimens in the back of the truck will go to be conditioned and bred up then returned to restock the oceans. It'll be valuable for you to see this end of our operation.' Meg smiled. 'Hey, maybe you'll recognise some of the fish you caught.'

'Yippee, a reunion,' said Sharly.

'And.' Meg smiled and wrapped an arm around Trin's shoulders. 'I called ahead for a booking at the medical centre, for you to have that scan. The centre isn't far from here, see the green sign?' She pointed down the street. 'It'll only take twenty minutes, tops, and it's no big deal, okay?' She gave Trin a quick hug and looked at Sharly, as if to say, *Make sure Trin gets the scan.* 'I can walk down there with you if you like.'

'End of the street ... sweet,' said Sharly. 'I got this.'

Meg nodded and sighed. 'After that, you guys can go and amuse yourselves for a while. I've got reports to hand in and then I'll head across to trade for some supplies.'

'How long before we need to be back?' asked Trin.

'Three, maybe four hours.' Meg pointed to the line of bubbling, black clouds. 'Then it should be party time.'

'We'll be here with our buckets, ready,' said Sharly. She smirked and saluted.

'I'll call and let them know you're on the way,' Meg said.

'Don't worry, Meg, I won't chicken out,' said Trin.

'I know, Fish.' Meg smiled stiffly.

'She won't,' said Sharly, as she linked arms with Trin and pulled her toward the medical centre.

Trin concentrated on walking and remembering to breath.

'So what do you see?' Trin asked the med-tech.

'A brain.' The tech smiled. 'Hold still.'

'Is there anything wrong?'

'My job is to do the scan and tell people to be patient, because our doctor will have to take a look at the scan and then send a report to your doctor. That's Meg, right?'

'Yeah.' Trin let out a shuddering breath.

'Sorry, Trin.' The med-tech held out her hand to help Trin up from the machine. 'I wish I could tell you more.'

'So does she get a lollypop for being a big brave girl?' Sharly asked the technician, who led Trin back to the front desk.

'Cut back, Sharls.' Trin elbowed Sharly and shoved her out the front door. 'Thank you,' she called over her shoulder towards the desk.

'Come on, girl, just a little humour. You know, you were looking pretty shackled as you went in.'

'Thanks, Sharls.' Trin blew out a long slow breath and stared at the ground.

'So, do you have burley for brains?'

'What?'

'Well, they looked into your head, did they find brains or just fish guts?'

'Frube.' Trin punched Sharly's arm.

'You're welcome.'

'They said they'd message the report to Meg when it's done.' Trin's stomach flipped, imagining what the report would say. She focused on remembering the sensation of wellness she'd felt at Lighthouse Island and her stomach calmed a little.

Sharly squeezed her into a hug. 'And it'll say that you're fine, except for the burley brain. Now let's do a crankin' tour of High and Dry.'

'Totally,' said Trin, shaking thoughts of the scan from her mind.

They walked out under the green-blue of the pre-storm sky into the dusty, bustling streets.

High and Dry, like all the sojourn settlements, had been put together in a hurry, so nothing was tall or shiny like the images they'd seen of New Canberra, or even Old Canberra, which was now New Sydney. The streets here were wide, and the centre of town was arranged in an efficient but unimaginative grid pattern that accommodated the essentials for the new city.

Away from the very centre, the rest of the city was a patchwork pieced together by refugees from all over the world. Each time Trin and Sharly turned into a new street, there were new sights and sounds, delicious smells, bursts of unexpected and amazing music, and talking, laughter, singing.

They tasted samples and brought food that they piled onto wooden meal trays. Their feasts teetered as they walked across to a paved area, with a sign that read UNITED NATIONS PARK. They sat eating under huge shade sails surrounded by displays about the founding of the settlements.

Sharly finished her meal first and walked around reading from the display boards. 'Did you know,' she called, 'that before the rising, the government used to try and limit the numbers of immigrant arrivals? But with low-lying cities and islands worldwide being inundated by the rising sea, the UN made a charter called the Convention on the Climate Refugee, then the rules all changed.'

Trin finished eating and started looking at the photos showing the migration history. 'Travelling in those cruise ships would've been okay, even if they were crowded, but can you imagine being out in a storm in that tiny fishing boat?' Trin ran her hand across the photo. 'It must've been so scary for them.'

'Hey, there's the aquarium.' Sharly pointed across the park to a low, blue building.

'Time for our reunion,' said Trin, smiling.

They entered the aquarium, where the dusty brightness of the streets was replaced by the cool blue-green light within. Trin breathed deeply and realised how much she was missing the smell of the sea and the salty moisture in the air.

There was a gaggle of squealing kids pressed up against the glass of a huge aquarium tank. They were watching, with wide, amazed eyes, all the fish swimming back and worth and looping past each other. When the fish nudged against the glass near their faces, the squeals exploded into shrieks.

'We're not going to see much with those guys here,' said Sharly.

'Probably not, but this place will be part of our job one day, I hope, so we should try and look around.'

A woman wearing a sandy-beige station uniform was heading towards them. 'Follow me, please,' she said pointing to a small door.

'We were just …' Trin began.

The woman tapped at her badge and pointed at the station ID badges Trin had forgotten she and Sharly were wearing. 'I'm Bon, I thought you might like a crowd-free experience of the breeding station.'

'Thanks. I'm Trin, and this is Sharly. We're fishers from Whitlam.'

'If you're from Whitlam, then thank you. We get quality specimens from you guys, and lots of them. You send us the highest numbers of viable stock for our anti-bloat program. Go through and have a look around without the crowds. Sorry I can't come with, but everyone is preparing for the festival so it's only me here today.'

'Thanks, Bon.'

They pushed through the door and stepped into a long, doomed tunnel of blue. Above them was huge arch of glittering water, crowded with fish.

Trin stared, pressing her hands against the cool glass. 'Outstanding.'

'Hi, guys,' said Sharly to the fish. 'It's crankin' to see you all again.' She nudged Trin's shoulder. 'You okay?'

'Yeah, I've just never seen so many fish in one place, except in the nets. And all these rays, and the urchins, amazing.' Trin stayed pressed up against the glass, just like the kids had been. She counted species and identified stuff she had never seen except for in computer files.

'Trin.'

'Yeah, what?'

'Trin … look up.'

Trin followed Sharly's gaze. On the other side of the glass arch, above her head, hundreds of fish had clustered together. They weren't feeding or fighting; they were just swirling around, forming a mandala of scales and tails above Trin's head.

'Crankin' girl, you're a fish whisperer.'

'Bail out, frube,' said Trin, startled by the scene. 'Very funny. What did you do?'

'Wasn't me.'

Trin walked away, further down the tunnel, and the fish followed her.

'Sharls.' Trin squeaked. 'What's happening?'

'Not sure.' Sharly laughed. 'It's your weird thing, not mine, girl, but it's crankin'.'

Trin stopped at the bend in the tunnel. The fish were still swirling above her like a silver cloud. Her heart was racing, but she realised that right now would be the only time to test her theory for sure. 'Sharls, you've got to promise not to say anything.'

'Hey, what's a friend for?'

Trin watched the fish swirling around above her. *Home*, she thought.

The swirling mass of fish thinned out, fanning away in all directions as they went back to their hiding places in the tank.

Trin gulped and caught her breath, then tried again. *Gather*.

In ones and pairs, the fish returned, forming a swirling mass above her and Sharly. This time, even the rays joined the congregation.

'You are legendary, Trin girl. Tennan would stop being such a quimby if he could see this.'

'You can't tell *anyone*, Sharls,'

'I already promised, Trin. I'm with you, whatever you need. But hey, can you do a few more tricks, just for me? What a show.'

Trin tried out a couple more tests, sending the strange school to various locations in the tank. She even sent them to visit the bunch of kids still pressed up against the glass at the outer wall of the tank. A squeal of delight rose up. Then Trin sent the school scattering before Bon could notice their unusual behaviour.

The fish followed Trin's directions over and over again. It was no coincidence, and this proof made her smile and shudder. She felt lightheaded, and her breath seemed caught in her lungs. It was really real, not just a theory or a hunch anymore.

Thank you—home, she signalled finally, and the fish went back to their territories in the tank. Trin watched them swim away as she slid down the wall of the tunnel and slumped on the floor.

Sharly gave her a big cup of water she had gotten from somewhere and Trin drank it slowly while she willed her pounding heart to slow down. *How can I be doing this?*

Sharly guided Trin back to the public viewing area. 'Thanks for letting us see back there,' she said to Bon.

Trin managed a tight smile, but she was struggling to speak.

Back outside the aquarium, the air was now filled with humidity and jumpy ions. They walked back through town under the green-black clouds, watching the storm roll into High and Dry. A cool, sticky wind whipped up, causing a dance of willy-willies up and down the wide streets.

Trin was calmer by the time they reached the Office of the Environment. They leaned on the truck and watched as the storm finished filling the sky.

Trin started counting the seconds between the knives of lightning in the distance and the boom of thunder. 'I calculate the storm's seven k's out,' she said, nudging Sharly.

'Yeah, the counting thing, love your scientific method, girl.' She licked her finger and held it up. 'Wind speed eighty k's per hour, from the northeast,' she scoffed.

'Cut back, Sharls.'

'Sorry, I know you love storms.'

'I love them more when they're rolling in over the ocean.'

'Unshackle. You're here now, so take a break from your ocean for a while, hey.'

'You mean, don't mention talking to fish.'

'Or herding them.' Sharly smiled. 'Just enjoy yourself. This festival's all about the monsoon, so everyone here must be as mad about storms as you are.'

'Enough with the "mad", okay?' She shoved Sharly extra hard, causing her to lose her balance and raise a puff of yellow dust as she hit the ground. Trin leaned over to help her up and a large cold splash of rain hit the back of her neck. It was festival time.

'Let's go,' Meg said, throwing the buckets at them.

They jumped in the truck and rolled up the windows as the raindrops started getting serious. Meg headed towards the party sounds that had just started up in the square in the centre of town. As they arrived, the skies opened up and the people of High and Dry let out raucous cheers of relief, hope, joy. The rain would let the city live for another year.

For the rest of the afternoon, everyone danced around in the rain, filled buckets with rainwater and poured them into the catcher troughs. The ground beneath their feet had turned from dust to a slippery, glutinous mud. Kids were sliding on their bellies through the yellow slick, squealing as they slid by.

The raindrops were cool and huge. Trin had never imagined she could get so wet without swimming in the ocean. At home, the storms were accompanied by tidal surges, and they were too severe to be outside in, so Trin had never really experienced a rainstorm up close like this.

Her skin was wrinkling and swelling, like she was a sponge soaking up all the water the storm threw at her. She noticed that Sharly wasn't puffing up, but Trin didn't get the chance to question it because the huge speakers started announcing something and everyone's attention turned to the main stage. The last of the day's light was fading and the crowd settled down to take part in the formal Monsoon Festival blessings.

'We know that in the other places we once used to call home, water sometimes meant death.' The gentle voice boomed out above the storm. 'But on this sacred day in High and Dry, water means life. Life for the crops and the livestock. Life for the citizens who came from near and far, and who now call this new and hopeful place home. Blessings and peace on us all.'

'Blessings and peace,' echoed the crowd as they reached to shake hands and hug their fellow citizens. Then the greetings morphed into the music of many languages, 'Blessings at *kapaya paan.*'

'Ngaahi tapaki me te rangimarie.'

'Ealayh alssalah walssalam.'

'Evolgie kai eirini.'

'Blessings and peace,' Meg whispered, squeezing Trin and Sharly into a soggy hug.

They stood in the darkness, under the roiling monsoon clouds, with the fusion reggae band on stage pumping out tunes above the din of the rain thumping on the metal roofs all around the city. The buckets were stacked into tall towers, and the good folk of High and Dry took to dancing in the joyous mud.

Regardless of the positive buzz all around her, Trin could not ignore the fact that she felt sick. She still felt puffy and swollen; her head hurt, and the party lights were melting into a coloured swamp as her head throbbed. Her muscles twitched and cramped, and she had to pee, again. How many times had that been since sunset?

'Are you okay?' asked Meg.

'Fine,' snapped Trin. 'Sorry, Meg, feeling a bit tired, I guess,' she lied.

'Probably time to call it a night,' Meg said gently. 'There's food waiting for us back at the dorms.'

'I'm starved,' said Trin, suddenly having a massive craving to eat something super-salty, something she only did when she was sick.

For dinner, Trin ate two huge, salty smoked fish and tossed a palm full of table salt into her mouth while no one was looking. Her head still ached and she felt nauseous, and she had to concentrate on keeping the salty fish in her stomach. Every muscle ached. She'd had these symptoms before. Her mother used to get similar symptoms, which is why Meg and her dad always went so kraken when she got sick.

Before Meg could notice anything, Trin made her excuses and went to her room. She peed for the fourth time since getting home. She flopped onto her bed feeling too sick to give any thought to her scan results. All she could think about was swimming in the ocean, but that wasn't an option right now. She fell into a restless sleep and dreamed of the wonderful salty sea.

THE BELOW

The black bubble containing the catalyst quivered in Rilla's palm. She placed it in her mouth and it squirmed across her tongue as if it had come to life. She swallowed. The slithering, black globule squirmed on the back of her tongue, but it remained there. She gagged and forced herself to swallow again. The bubble of potion bulged then elongated, some of it remaining in her mouth while the rest stretched downward, blocking her throat. Then, at the back of her tongue, the burning started.

Her body convulsed as she instinctively tried to regurgitate the putrid glob back out again. Holding her hands tightly over her mouth and swallowing doubly hard, she felt the misshapen bubble burst in her throat. A hot, foul bitterness rose into her nose and down towards her stomach. Then it radiated out along her gill veins and into her lungs. The putrid heat sunk deep into her belly, burning like the lava that disgorged from the vents.

A buzzing, screeching wail exploded in her mind, as though every neume from every Abrax had stormed into her head all at once.

Rilla could feel one neume rising above the tumult: *Your journey is begun, Rilla. You're a new changeling now. You're no longer of this place. Ascend. Ascend.*

Pelagya blurred back into view, her tired face pale with distress. *You must ascend. Now!*

Rilla remembered that the catalyst would take time to rend the changes that would turn her from Abrax into a walker. This time was set long ago, to match the length of time it took to ascend from the Deeps to the surface.

Ascend. Pelagya embraced Rilla tightly, then released her and, with unnatural strength, pushed her up towards the Above.

Rilla felt the resistance as she was forced through the water. Plunging upwards away from the vents, the water quickly became icy and thick. The glowing circle of the kelp forest diminished below her, and she kicked her tails hard and swam into the growing darkness. She looked upward through an endless cold blackness towards the Above. Pelagya had told her it was morning in the Above, and that it would take her until the sun was setting to ascend to the Between, the area between the shallows and the shoreline.

Her transformation had begun in the Deeps and would finish in the waters of the Between.

Rilla swam on. The burning from the catalyst was cooled by the frigid blackness of the Deeps. In the darkness, she could see nothing but the dim glow of her own fear, pale across her skin. All she could do was trust that her instincts were guiding her up. If not, she could swim across the sea and be lost in the open ocean and eaten, or, worse, she could stumble back to Lemuria.

The water slowly turned from black to darkest blue. She was moving upward. The ruckus of neumes inside her head quieted. The burning had been replaced with an intense aching in her fins and arms, caused by the endless effort of swimming upward. The movement of her tails, so familiar all her life, had begun to feel unnatural, as though they were not fully hers to control. The water she had swum in all her life was starting to feel like a strange place to her.

Rilla knew the surface was still a long way above her, but she was sure the catalyst was already making changes.

She struggled on, not daring to pause and rest her aching body even for a moment. The ocean was lightening around her and the water was growing warmer. She fixed her eyes on the distant glow of the sun.

I've done it!

She was energised, and swam harder as she watched all the brightening blues ripple and flicker around her. Then the blues suddenly faded as her vision was blocked.

Tentacles. Kraken.

A massive tangled cloud had wrapped around her face and arms. She could see nothing, but she felt the tangle slither across her skin. Her body tingled with panic and she lashed out at the snarled mass. She ripped at the tendrils that surrounded her, ready to fight this creature when it moved in closer.

Their eyes are their weakest point. I'll jab at its eyes.

She stiffened. Despite the catalyst, her blood had turned to ice. She waited for the thicker tentacles to roll across her body, showing her that the kraken was close enough for her to stab at its eyes. Then she could escape as it plumed itself in a black ink cloud. But the thicker tentacles did not coil around her.

This thing is not a kraken.

Rilla stopped and forced herself to clear her vision so she could make sense of what was happening. When she pulled the long tendrils away from her eyes, she could see they were her cirrus; she was surrounded by a tangled cloud of her own cirrus. It had fallen away from her head and body, as Pelagya had said it would, and it had tangled around her. This was the first sign that real changes had started.

She looked at the lifeless tendrils in her hands. *Perhaps some of these will float down and be a message to Pelagya.* She released them and watched as they drifted downward.

Curious, Rilla dared to investigate what else the catalyst had done so far. She felt her head; it was bare and smooth. The skirt of cirrus at her gird was also completely gone, but she could see no other changes. Turning back to the light, she willed her tails to move and pushed on towards the surface.

Indigo water faded to cobalt, lapis, cerulean. Rilla was slowing, weakening. She chanced a look down at her body. Her fins looked smaller.

But I'm still so deep. Surely I should be closer to the shallows by now.

Her tails fought against the currents.

The sea has changed, swollen.

She gulped at the water, trying to draw it in faster through her shrinking gills. Then she realised: the ancient makers of the catalyst had not reckoned on the changes brought to the sea by the warming and the frozen water melting. The seas were deeper now, so the distance up to the shallows was further.

Rilla struggled up through azure, sapphire, teal. Her mind was fizzing. Her gills and her fins continued to shrink. She watched as a long curl of pearlescent skin peeled away from her arm and twisted in the current. All along her arms, her body and her tails, the pale curls lifted loose and fluttered away into the blue. Her newly exposed skin was pale; there was no longer luminous colour there to match her neume. This new skin was thin, and she felt the cold seeping into her bones.

She looked up again and saw the slightest glimmers of sunlight reflecting on the water. Her shrivelled gills fizzed with joy. Soon she would reach the Above. With renewed hope, Rilla pushed upward again.

She could feel her bones grating against each other inside her tails, which were stiffening, already changing into walker legs. Her fins had almost completely shrivelled away.

Will my gills close before I get there?

Without the powerful strokes of her tail fins to propel her along, the current menaced Rilla, pushing her down and sideways, moving her away from her true course. She twisted to correct her slow upward bearing. Now her arms burned with the extra effort of having to claw through the water the way she had seen walkers swim. She was quickly becoming a stranger to her own blue sea. Her heart pounded in her ears. She saw splotchy colour on her eyelids, then her mind started to blacken.

My gills. I'm not there yet.

Rilla flipped her exhausted body over. If she were going to perish here and not reach the Above, she would look up at the sky one last time.

The jittering surface of the water was speckled with uncountable tiny suns. The glinting points of light blurred and mixed with the black splotches in Rilla's fading vision. The Between would claim her, but she did not regret her decision.

Light and dark and colour swirled and then faded.

The coolness of the breeze roused Rilla as her face broke through the jewelled surface of the water. She gasped hungrily to fill her lungs with cool, delicious air. She dropped back down below the surface and struggled up for more air. Without her tail fins, she had to slice her arms back and forth through the water to stop herself from sinking again.

As she struggled to learn to swim with her new walker body, she watched the bright blue of the daytime sky fading to orange-pink. This was the first sunset of her new life in the Above.

The air chilled her face and shoulders. She folded her arms across herself to protect against the cold and kicked furiously to keep her face above the water. She felt the raised lines that were all that remained of where her gills had been. It was done; she was a walker now, or would be, once she had taught herself to walk.

The sky was quickly darkening. She needed shelter from the growing cold. She thought of her nest and Neeva, so far below, and her eyes pained as they did when she felt hurt. Warm water came from her eyes and flowed slowly down her face, mixing with the sea. Pelagya had warned that there would be some corporeal pain, but it wasn't her body hurting her now.

This was her soul paining at the loss of love, the loss of family.

Rilla never wanted to see her father again after learning of the cruelty he and the Gathering of Colours had inflicted on Pelagya and her daughter. She thought of all the half-alive weed-creatures sorrowing because of the orders given by her father and the elders. Though she didn't regret her choice, she grieved at never seeing her mother or Neeva again.

As the pain water streamed down her face, she made a new noise. Not the huffing sound that was laughing, but a plaintive wailing like the call of a lonely bird. It rose from deep within her in jolting sobs. Her heart ached as she wailed and she slid back under the water.

Maybe I should let the sea have me.

Finally, Rilla pushed the grief away and filled the space in her heart with determination.

'I'm here now. This is my home.' She spoke out loud with air-words, but neumed *doubt—fear*. She looked at her arms, expecting the silty, purple of fear to show on her skin. Then she remembered that her old skin had been shed as she ascended. Her new skin showed a tinge of luminescence, only the palest imitation of her old Abrax colours.

Her chill deepened.

I'll need a new nest. She scanned the shore and watched the last day bird swoop across, low in the sky, heading for the island. This rocky place was near the shore and it had a walker nest on it that appeared deserted. The structure was tall and proud, and reminded her of the Hall of Colours in Lemuria, but it didn't seem to be grown from coral; it was somehow crafted by the walkers.

The bird landed at the very top of the tower. It ruffled its feathers, settled down into its nest and neumed *contentment—safety.*

The water darkened around her and grew colder. Rilla watched the larger walker nest further along the rocks. It had started glowing and quieting. No such glow came from the tower on the island, and Rilla had never seen any walker go there, so she decided that this place would be her new nest, at least until she became a real walker. Exhausted, she flipped over onto her back and sculled towards the island.

A new and fierce burning began deep within her. She cried out, and the startled bird, up in the tower, squawked in response. Rilla felt like there was lava, from the vents of the Deeps, burning within her. Every movement made her bones bubble with fire. She thought she could hear her bones rasping, grating against each other, as she swam the last small distance to the island.

At the shore, she reached out and placed her hand on the land. As she did, the skin on her hand burned with a new intensity. Pelagya had told her to expect discomfort, but she had said nothing about this burning and pain.

Rilla cursed her, but how could Pelagya have known? No Abrax had ever returned to tell about the change.

Rilla lay at the water's edge, breathing hard. She watched the moon rise until her bones finally cooled. Now each lungful of night air chilled her to the core. She needed to be inside the tall nest, sheltered from the night winds. As she crept up onto the island's gritty beach, each part of her new skin that came in contact with the land burned and stung. Pain water flowed from her eyes as she pulled herself up the slope.

Gradually she learned how to bend her tails—legs—in the middle, and managed to lift her body up off the sand. Now the burning was only on her hands and where her legs scraped across the beach.

The moon was high when she reached the tall, narrow entrance to the nest cave. The fire on her skin was fading. Determined to walk into her new nest, she gripped the square rocks at the entrance to the cave and pulled herself up.

She felt so heavy and awkward since leaving the water. She was slow, clumsy. Now, trying to pull herself upright, she felt as though some mystical force was trying to pull her back into the earth. Why hadn't the catalyst given her the strength the walkers must have to move against this pulling force with such ease?

Finally, she stood. Her tails no longer had fins, but instead stubby walker feet. Her bones crackled under the burden of her body's weight pressing down through her legs.

She wobbled and gripped the stones harder, wondering if the weight pushing down to her new feet might push her all the way into the ground. She inhaled a cold breath and stepped inside. Leaning heavily on the circular wall of the nest-cave, she managed a few more burning steps and collapsed onto a pile of something soft and slept.

After three days the burning had faded, but the catalyst continued to work its changes for many more days still. Each change made Rilla more like a walker, but the catalyst only changed her physical form. Without her determination, she would have simply lain on the shore like a seal out of water.

She had to teach herself to move on the land, crawling for many days before she gained the strength and balance to stand and move around her island like a true walker.

Even though swimming with walker feet instead of fins was challenging, the sea was still a great comfort to her, and she returned there daily to stretch her rigid limbs and hunt for food. Swimming was slow and difficult now, but she discovered that her gills were not fully sealed, only shrivelled. Though inefficient, they could still gather a little air from the sea. It was impossible to dive for too long, but still, having gills made hunting for fish easier.

As the days turned into weeks, Rilla spent much of her time watching and listening to the walkers as they worked around their nest. She especially watched Marcus.

It felt like eons ago that she had hidden in the boat's shadow and shared his neumes of concern for the sickness of the fish and the sea. He had such great plans and dreams to heal the damage.

The walkers spent so much time on the water that Rilla could easily observe them, gaining understanding of their ways and learning more of their air-words. She reached out for even the slightest neume, which gave her deeper insights that would help her be accepted as a walker when the time came. She hoped that time would be soon because she was lonely and wanted so badly to join them, but she urged herself to be patient. She needed to wait and make thorough preparations.

Regardless of the all the changes that the catalyst had caused, Rilla knew she still did not look enough like a walker. Her skin was very pale, and a slight, pearly glimmer remained. The skirt of cirrus around her gird had fallen away in the sea and not grown back again. The cirrus on her head had regrown quickly, but had changed and now looked like coarse walker hair. The long strands of her new hair didn't flutter about in the breeze like walker hair, but tended to clump into thick spiralling tendrils. She could keep it from roping together if she combed her fingers through the strands regularly.

She worried that anyone she met would immediately see that she was something else.

Venturing across the channel to the walker nest, which she now knew was called a station, she took cloth skins from where they were hung to dry and covered herself as the walkers did. The cloth scratched and burned her skin until she was used to it.

She focused on the scientists that neumed most strongly. She learned quickly about their science and how they perceived their plans and experiments. Regardless of the dangers of the unpredictable and enormous storm surges, these walkers stayed at this place and tried hard to learn the extent of the harm their kind had caused to the sea and the creatures that lived there. They were committed to making reparation.

Rilla dreamed of neuming with her father, to show him that the walkers were working hard to heal Mother Ocean. She was sure, now more than ever, that if the walkers and the Abrax could work together and share their knowledge and skills, the sea would be healed far sooner.

She could no longer descend to Lemuria as a messenger, but she could start working on the healing. As she waited for the catalyst to make its last changes, she studied the shoreline, the shallows around the station and the headland, watching fish movements and tasting the sea to measure the changes in salinity.

The clothes no longer burned her skin, and moving with them on her body was less awkward, so she wore them each day when she went out to study the shoreline. Looking at her reflection in a rock pool one day, she self-consciously combed her fingers through her ropey, sand-coloured hair.

Surely it was now time to chance approaching the walkers. She had learned many of their words, and her knowledge of walker science had grown. She had discovered a very vital thing: there were many more science stations like this one. Rilla planned to say that she was from one of these other stations, a visitor. Then she could visit these walkers, work with them, and get closer to Marcus.

Rilla walked along the southern side of the headland, sensing the movement of fish as they schooled around seeking food. She was caught up in their neumes and wasn't aware of Marcus until it was too late to hide from him.

She stared into his face. Panic flooded her with a rush of heat.

The fish neumed her panic and jittered in the water before fleeing to their hiding places in the rock crevices.

He will see my skin. She hurriedly rolled down the sleeves of her station shirt, and sent a neume to make him see her skin as walker gold-brown. She combed her hair smooth with shaky fingers.

'Hello.' Marcus looked shocked, but Rilla felt him neume: *pink—orange, happy—curious.* 'I didn't realise we had new team members arriving. I'm Marcus.'

He reached out one hand, Rilla mimicked the action, and they touched. A strange, sparking jolt passed between them, and their hands lingered for a delightful moment before they moved apart.

'Hello, I'm Rilla, and I'm not officially here.' She tried to calm her breathing and choose the correct air-words. She neumed strongly: *Believe me. Trust me.*

Marcus winced and rubbed his temples.

'I've heard so much about the work you're all doing here that I had to come and see for myself … and learn from you … and share what I know, if you think my knowledge is valuable.'

'Which station are you from?' *Trust—believe.*

Her lungs squeezed.

Mawson? he neumed.

'Mawson,' she stammered. 'I'm just staying for the season.'

'Wow, that's a long way to come.' *Doubt.*

Trust me. 'I was going home to … Sojourn Five … so I detoured back to the coast … I was curious.' She smiled and shrugged. *Believe me.*

'Well, Rilla, welcome to Whitlam Station,' he said. 'We're only small and just starting our research, so an extra set of hands is always welcome. I'll show you around.'

THE ABOVE

The trip back to the station felt long, torturously long. The truck was fully loaded with supplies, so they drove at half speed compared to the drive out. For most of the trip Trin stared at her feet, concentrating on not throwing up.

All she had thought about since she had woken the morning after the festival was the sea. For two days she had craved the salty ocean in a way she didn't think was possible. When Sharly had seen Trin sneaking salt to eat at breakfast that morning, Trin had made her promise to keep her secret. Sharly had helped to hide

Trin's sickness from Meg on the ride home by asking questions that she knew would start Meg on one of her rants or micro-lessons.

When Trin felt the first jolts from the ruts on the station access road, she was elated, but by then Sharly had run out of distractions.

Meg saw that something wasn't right. 'Not feeling well, Fish?'

'I'm just travel sick, Meg,' Trin said. 'I don't think I'm good in the truck.'

'You're not good at faking, either, Trin.' Meg shook her head. 'How long have you been sick?'

'Only since last night. Too much monsoon partying and exotic food, I think.

'The festival food was crankin',' Sharly added. 'And we ate loads of it.'

Trin nodded. 'I'm fine. I just want to have a swim.'

'A swim sounds great,' Sharly said, as the truck sighed to a stop next to the garden.

'You're kidding me, right?' Meg said. 'Nice try, guppies, but no swimming. Trin, you head down to the sickbay, now.'

'Please, Meg, not the sickbay. If Dad sees I'm sick he'll go all kraken on me again.'

Meg stared at her for a long moment. 'Okay, I'll tell him you two are unloading the truck, but get some rest. I'll get unpacked and then I'll check in on you, do some tests. Sharly, you make sure she gets to bed.'

'Yes, Meg.' Sharly grabbed both of their gear bags out of the truck.

Trin went to take a spare harness from the gardens then decided she didn't have the energy to snake down, so she walked slowly along the cliff edge to the closest ladder. The tantalising smell of the salty water filled her nostrils as she plodded down the stairs. Stopping when she reached the ladder junction at their cave, she took a long breath of salty air deeply into her lungs, exhaled slowly, turned away from the cave and kept on descending.

'I think you missed your exit,' said Sharly from behind her.

'I've got to swim,' rasped Trin.

'Meg will—'

'Don't care.' Trin trudged down the stairs.

'Burley!' Sharly mumbled. She shoved the bags into their cave and followed Trin down.

When she reached the shoreline, Trin stepped off the rocks fully dressed and flopped face down into the cool, salty water. She paddled her arms back and forth, pushing downwards against her own buoyancy to keep herself submerged for as long as possible. Looking down through the blue at the patterns of refracted sunlight rippling below her, she listened as the voices from the sea began to whisper inside her head again.

She flipped over and looked up from below at the glimmering surface of the water. It was like a liquid silver roof on her private haven. Staying under until her lungs were quaking for air, she felt a strange pressure, nearly pain, around her throat and collarbones.

She finally allowed herself to return to the surface. Bobbing up reluctantly and floating on the wavelets, she listened to the fish chatter, and a more distant something … a voice? It was the one she had heard in the water and on Lighthouse Island. She realised she felt pleased. Whatever this voice was, she was glad it was still there.

Sharly kept a nervous lookout for Meg while Trin splashed around. 'You cool?' she asked, as she held out a hand and pulled Trin back onto the rock ledge.

'Yeah. Yeah, I really am.' Trin smiled. 'I feel excellent.'

'Well, you better get to the cave before Meg catches you or you might not stay excellent.'

'I got rid of the evidence, all your wet clothes are in the machine with the other stuff,' said Sharly as she clambered through the cave mouth. 'Are you still feeling excellent?'

'Crankin'. I just needed a swim. Now all I need to do is to pass all Meg's tests and convince her it was only travel sickness.'

'And was it?'

'It doesn't matter what it was, does it, because I'm cool now. And I'm sick of talking about being sick, okay, *Meg*?'

'Sorry,' said Sharly.

'Hey, there are those weird guys, Kayn and Andy.' Trin pointed down at the pair standing at the water's edge.

'Watch them … wait.' She stared at them, hoping she'd see them change, like she had on the evening when they first arrived. She was convinced it was just a matter of time, and this time she would show Sharly. 'There. See it?'

'See what, Trin? They're just checking the readings on the sal gauges.'

'No, watch them, they sort of melted away. Then they were sort of shimmery and …'

'So, do they look shiny again like you said they did on the night they arrived?' Sharly teased. 'They look a bit knock-kneed to me. You know, you stand like that sometimes, too.'

'Forget about my knees, or their knees, Sharls. Surely you can see what they look like.' Trin smouldered with frustration and self-doubt.

'Hey, I didn't mean to stir you up. I'm just a bit worried about you, girl.' Sharly put her arm around Trin's shoulder and froze. 'I see it, the shubee thing.'

'What do you see?'

'They look faded, see-through, and for a second they sort of blended in with the water,' whispered Sharly.

'Keep watching, Sharly, and describe every detail to me. I need to know I'm not going crazy.' Trin turned to look at Sharly and her friend's arm slipped from her shoulder.

'It's gone, they look normal again,' Sharly said. 'I must've imagined it.'

Trin could still see the translucent, wavering forms of the men. 'You can't have imagined it.' She grabbed Sharly's hand and held it. 'Look again, Sharls.'

'No way. Nice trick. Can you tell what I'm thinking, too? That's crankin'!'

'It's not a trick.' An acid storm brewed in Trin's stomach.

'Yeah. It must be something like the fish-talk thing. You're putting images in my mind.'

'It's not a trick,' Trin insisted.

'Trin, girl, I saw you do the signal thing with the fish, so why not people, too?'

'I'm not making it up.'

'But there can't be creepy blue guys visiting Whitlam Station, because there's no such thing as creepy blue guys.'

'But it all looks so real.' Trin sighed and stared at Kayn and Andy, struggling to make sense of the images. They remained the same shape, but they flickered between dressed and undressed; hats, then blue-green dreadlocks. Trin was expecting to see scales as she struggled to focus her eyes, but instead she saw smooth, pearled leathery skin that reflected the colours around them. They had more of the dreadlock things around their hips.

Trin sobbed. 'I'm a freak.'

'Hey, girl, unshackle, okay?' Sharly turned Trin to face her. 'There've been lots of changes caused by the rising and the warming. We don't know the effects they're having on lots of species. They could be affecting us, too. These weird things might just be a transition to something, like the beginning of something new that will be normal for us one day. Some of it might be imagination, but you're sending signals to fish, and now maybe even me. Kudos.' Sharly produced her goofiest smile. 'And you're only knock-kneed when you're tired.'

Trin punched Sharly and the storm in her stomach started to calm itself. She couldn't be angry with Sharly for not believing what was happening when Trin didn't really believe it herself.

Kayn and Andy finally looked up, and when they noticed Trin and Sharly they waved. Trin felt an aching pressure inside her head, and the rippling images faded. Once again the visitors became tanned and clothed.

Trin rubbed the dull pain away and wondered what the scan report would say.

THE BELOW

Rilla stayed at Whitlam Station for the season, and lingered on until the season had become a year. The catalyst had not made any changes to her body for many moons, and she knew it had stopped short of transforming her completely into a walker. Her skin remained pale and slightly iridescent. Her hair often looked damp and ropey. She covered these physical anomalies by contriving strong neumes that she projected into the minds of all those at the station, ensuring that Marcus and the others would see her only as she wished them to see her.

Though she was occasionally troubled with bouts of a mysterious sickness, Rilla became a valuable member of the team at the station. She worked on various projects, sharing insights about the sea that only she could know. Because of her contributions to the research, the projects progressed quickly and the data gathered was sound, at times groundbreaking.

Marcus and Rilla spent most of their off-duty time together. He taught her a traditional and, in her opinion, very ineffective method of catching fish, using metal hooks and string suspended from a pole.

'You always seem to cast the line right on their heads,' said Marcus, as he watched Rilla pull in another fish.

'That's a good thing,' Rilla smiled, 'otherwise we'd have to eat with the others in the dining hall instead of out here alone, together-alone.' She gutted and cleaned the fish while Marcus started the fire. Rilla didn't care too much for fish that had been cooked, but she was enthralled by the sight of the dancing licks of flame that burst from driftwood, which only moments before had been lying inert on the rocks.

'You stare at those flames like you've never seen fire,' Marcus said.

'It's just so beautiful. It's like the sun has been captured and imprisoned within the ring of stones.'

'I love listening to the way you describe things. You make everything sound so miraculous.'

'It's how it is to me.' Rilla turned back to watch the flames. These times spent alone out on the headland were delightful. Away from the clamour of the mumbling neumes generated by the other walkers at the station, Marcus and Rilla neumed without distraction. Though Marcus wasn't conscious of the link between their minds, Rilla knew they shared a deep and unique connection that bound them to each other. Seeking out this type of connection was the way the Abrax found the one they would join with for their life partnership.

Although Rilla neumed strongly to all the walkers to ensure her true nature wasn't discovered, she considered it a necessary dishonesty, and she took care not to control Marcus's thoughts or feelings about her in any other way. She wanted their connection to be true. One day she would explain it all to him, when the time was right.

Life at the station became familiar and rhythmic. Rilla and Marcus learned much about the sea and each other, and slowly their love blossomed. On the twentieth moon after her ascension, the walkers of the station gathered together to celebrate the joining of Rilla and Marcus.

As the leader of the small station community, Meg held responsibilities for many aspects of station life. She was the certified representative of the government, and when duty called, she set aside her scientific work to attend to staff welfare, policy directives and record keeping. Today she had the joyous duty of officiating at Marcus and Rilla's joining ceremony.

Usually station staff records were well maintained, but Meg hadn't been too worried when Rilla said she was missing some records and personal papers. Lost information wasn't uncommon. With the disruptions weather events caused with uploads to the official archives, sometimes personal records were incomplete.

Rilla took this belief about the frailties of the technology as an opportunity and she neumed a strong urging that compelled Meg to use her authority as station leader to amend the civic records. When Meg was finished making the guided adjustments, Rilla had gained a bona fide walker identity, and her joining to Marcus was noted in the civic records. She was now truly a walker.

The moon was full, and the sea surrounding the peninsula and the island sparkled with a million speaks of moonlight. The fire crackled as Rilla and Marcus shared their meal of fish.

'It's been five moons since our joining,' Rilla said quietly.

'It's our five-moon-iversary and I didn't get you a gift.' Marcus laughed and hugged her.

'I have a gift for both of us … a child.'

She watched the moonlight sparkle in his eyes as he stared at her. 'A child.' He stammered. *Joy—amazement—delight.*

She joined in his neume of happiness, but her own joy and amazement was tinged with a secret sense of dread. Of course there could be a baby, the Abrax and the walkers were the same species under the skin. They had both started life deep in the oceans. It was just that they had taken two different evolutionary tracks because of the catalyst. Yes, there would be a child, but what would this halfling child look like?

Rilla knew the catalyst had halted before her change was complete. Would her baby need to breathe air, or would it gulp through gills, or perhaps some third thing she could not begin to envisage?

What have I done?

THE ABOVE

'Surprise!' Trin slid a gift box of chocolates across the lab bench. 'I know they're your favourites.'

'Thanks, Fish, how did you like High and Dry?'

'We had a great time, but I missed you.' Trin hugged her father. 'See you at dinner.' She headed for the sickbay. Since the swim, she was feeling great and all the swelling had gone away.

Trin was calling it 'rain sickness'. She knew it was real. She had searched the archives for her symptoms and found that they matched something called 'water intoxication'. She had experienced most of the symptoms, but none of the causes that were listed in the files. Apparently it was caused by consuming huge amounts of water. Because of all the spicy food they ate at High and Dry, she had been drinking more water than she normally did at home, but nowhere near the quantities described in the research.

How weird to get sick from too much water, she thought. Her hands and feet had become swollen from the rain, but she swam in the sea all the time and it never happened then. And although everyone else had got really wet as well, she was the only one left puffy, bloated and weak.

'Hi, Meg, I was just catching up with Dad and thought I'd save you the trip up the ladder.' Trin walked into the sickbay, making sure she sounded extra chirpy.

'You look great.'

'I felt awesome after I had a ... shower and some lunch. Then I even did some study,' she added for effect.

Meg smiled and shook head. 'It seems you've bounced back, but I still want to do a quick check.'

'Cool.'

Meg mumbled to herself as she poked and prodded, checked and measured. After a few minutes she gave Trin a final all-clear from the travel sickness.

'Has the scan report come yet?'

'Not yet.' There was an alert tone from Meg's computer.

'Go check if this is it,' said Trin, crossing her fingers.

Meg walked across and sat reading something on the screen. She turned to face Trin and her smile said everything Trin needed to know.

'All good?'

Meg nodded.

'Cowabunga!' Trin felt an unexpected wave of joy join her own. She flung her arms wide and did a goofy, happy dance. Grabbing Meg, she made her join in. When Trin released Meg, she saw her quickly wipe away a tear.

'So, anything else on your mind?' said Meg, returning to her cheery doctor tone. 'Pardon my pun.'

'Groan,' said Trin. 'Yeah, one thing. What makes a person knock-kneed?'

'Well, that's a shift of topic.' Meg shrugged. 'You're only slightly knock-kneed, Fish. Your mum was a bit that way as well. She had weak ankles, and she must have passed on the trait to you. We can do something if you want, different shoes ...'

'No, that's okay. I noticed that the new guys look a bit that way, too. I just wondered why it happens.' She shrugged the conversation away. 'No big deal.'

'Speaking of the new guys, Andy and Kayn are really interested in talking to the fishers. They're very impressed with the success you're having with the big catches.'

'Sure.' Trin swallowed hard at the idea of being close to Kayn and Andy. Now that her scan had come back clear, it meant the weird things she had seen were not hallucinations. She thought about Sharly's theory about the sea affecting them, but that didn't make things feel any less weird. 'How can we help?'

'They mentioned plans for a tag-and-release project to help them gather data.'

'Sounds fine. Does that mean I'm allowed to swim now?' She smiled, pleased that she hadn't been caught swimming this morning.

'Yes, Trin. Will you guys be fishing today? I'll get Andy and Kayn to meet you at the net shed. What time?'

'We probably have enough daylight to cast the net … high tide's in an hour.'

'You always know the tides, Trin, even though we've been away at High and Dry.'

'I'd be a bad fisher if I didn't know the tides, Meg. Get them to meet us at the net shed and they can explain what they want. But tell them they'll have to help us gut the ones they don't want for their project. That's the team rules.'

'You're expecting a catch today, then?'

'You never know,' said Trin, as she headed out of the sickbay. But she did know. Even away from the water, she could feel the activity out there. This afternoon the nets would be full.

A tangle of net was spread across the flat rock in front of the storage shed. The fishers sat around the edges looking for holes.

'Hello, Mal. Can we help you with the repairs?' asked Andy as he and Kayn approached.

'Thanks,' said Mal. 'Andy, Kayn, this is Sharly and Trin, they were away for a few days.

'It's good to finally meet you,' said Andy to the girls.

'You know everyone else,' added Mal.

'Raz, Tennan and Nix,' said Andy, a little too formally.

Kayn didn't speak; he just nodded his head stiffly as Andy said each name.

Tennan snickered and there was an outbreak of comic nods all round.

Trin wasn't surprised Mal was already so chummy with Andy and Kayn. Getting a choice study spot at the station to do their field Internships was a big deal for both of them. Mal was as keen as she was to gain credits towards their applications. He'd probably already logged all the contact time he'd had with Kayn and Andy into his journal on the ed-net. While Trin had been sneaking to Lighthouse Island to chase weird voices and dancing at the Monsoon Festival, Mal had been making valuable contacts.

She cringed at the idea of having to leave the sea and go inland to study. The two new researchers looked fine right now, so she needed to ignore the visions of weird blue dreadlocks and work with them. Maybe she and Sharly had just been spooked and let their imaginations get out of control. Then she thought about the signals. They had seemed so real.

'Find a spot around the net somewhere,' Trin told them, 'and check for fish-sized holes.' She threw some short pieces of carbon twine towards Kayn. 'Use the twine to tie up the holes.'

'Thank you,' said Kayn. He sat near her and reached out to shake her hand. 'The others have said that this team's success with fishing is because of your ability to ... read the sea.'

'I suppose you could say that.' Trin sniffed; Kayn smelt acrid, fishy, briny. Strange, but familiar. 'I think fishing is mostly good luck.'

'She's being modest,' said Raz. 'She hardly ever has any bad fishing days, especially lately.'

'Well, that's what we need,' said Andy. 'The more fish we can tag, the better our data profile will be.'

'So, Trin, are you planning to work in this field when you've studied?' asked Kayn.

'Of course, I couldn't imagine being anywhere else.'

'And ocean science runs her family,' said Raz. 'Trin's parents both work, um, worked here.' Raz sucked a breath and flashed an apologetic look at Trin.

'Both your parents?' Kayne said. 'I met your dad ... in the lab.'

'Yeah, Mum and Dad worked together studying the effects of salinity changes way back before I was born.' Trin squirmed at little. 'Mum died when I was very young.'

'Was there an accident?' Kayn leaned in close to her, and then checked himself and backed away stiffly. 'Sorry, I didn't mean to pry. It's just that you achieve tremendous things at this station, very efficient methods, but the work is so filled with risk, and I presumed ...'

'I think you've drifted a bit off topic,' said Sharly, being defensive on Trin's behalf.

Trin felt a pressure behind her eyes; a third, different mental signal was pushing at her mind, but it lasted only a second and then she sensed it being pushed away. At that moment, she noticed Andy give Kayn a quick, narrow-eyed glance and Kayn dropped his eyes back to the net.

Trin was trying hard to ignore the weirdness, as she had promised herself. 'We should get the net in the water now,' was all she said.

'Why? What have you noticed?' said Andy, a little too excitedly.

'Well, like you said, I can read the sea.' Trin stared knowingly at the water, hiding a smile. 'I noticed that the tide's turning, so the fish will be active now.'

'That's it?' asked Kayn. 'There's nothing else?'

Trin felt a sudden flash of annoyance. 'Oh, yeah, didn't I tell you, I talk to the fish, and they tell me how they're feeling and where they're running.' She glared at Tennan, who took the hint and had sense enough to keep his mouth shut.

'Do you want some fish to tag or not?' she said to Kayn, hauling the net towards the water.

'Of course,' said Andy. 'I'll go and get our equipment.'

'Should I help you with the net?' asked Kayn.

He looked like he'd never fished before. Trin sighed. These guys seemed to be getting weirder, but at least they weren't fading to blue and turning all nude and shiny. Maybe it had just been her imagination, or nerves and panic because of the scan.

'No,' she said to Kayn. 'Thanks, but we'll handle the nets. You get ready to tag or grab a knife, and rip guts. We'll have your fish really soon.'

She hooked the net onto the clip on her wetskin and jumped off the rock shelf, heading out through the swell with easy, powerful strokes. Once in the water, she heard the chittering of the schools' direction signals and knew exactly where she needed to be to fill the nets. She heard that other signal again, too, and glanced briefly towards Lighthouse Island.

She shook the whisper out of her head. This afternoon had to be all about impressing Kayn and Andy so she could get onto their project team. She set out towards the schooling fish and the team followed her lead, pulling the net into position.

'Put all the guts and heads in the bucket,' said Trin, watching Andy and Kayn slitting the fish clumsily, like first-time fishers. 'You really don't catch many fish at your station, do you? Or do you have someone else do the cleaning for you?'

'We don't—'

'Watch that blade,' Andy interrupted, and glared at Kayn for a moment.

'We deal with our food fish slightly differently, yes,' said Andy.

'Thank you for sacrificing so many of your food fish so we could tag them for our project,' said Kayn. 'Though I guess you'll get plenty more tomorrow.'

'We will if Trin's around,' said Tennan, flinging a long string of guts up into the air. The seagulls ignited into a screeching mid-air tug of war.

'Would you be willing to help us with more of our work, Trin?' Andy asked. 'We'd appreciate tapping into your knowledge of this place, and it would contribute to your science studies.'

Trin noticed Mal bristle. She knew how much being on this project would mean to him, and to Sharly. 'I'd like Mal and Sharly involved as well. We've been helping each other with our studies for a long time and we work well together.' She saw a questioning look pass between Andy and Kayn.

'Yes,' said Andy. 'If that's the way you need it to be, we can change our … plans to suit this new situation.'

'So what do you want us to do?'

'We'd like you go guide us when we dive. We'd like to look at the rock reef that runs around that outcropping.' Kayn pointed at the peninsula.

'Snorkelling, you mean,' said Trin. 'Meg won't let anyone dive here unless she's trained them herself, and we're *definitely* not allowed.'

'Well, we're experienced divers, yes, but we're happy to abide by your station's regulations. Snor-kelling will be acceptable,' said Andy.

'Is tomorrow's high tide soon enough?' asked Mal.

'That'll be fine.'

THE BELOW

Motherhood rituals were an empowering tradition shared among Abrax females. Celebrations of females and mothers and babies happened for many days before a youngling was born, and were signalled by the preborn reaching out with its neumes to all females in the mother's circle.

Before this reaching out, the neumes between mother and preborn remained private as the youngling grew. The neumes were strong, and allowed mother and youngling to create a deep bond. When the preborn was almost ready to enter the sea, it neumed broadly, reaching out to all the mature females in the mother's circle. Young females who were approaching maturity would also receive the preborn neume, and be celebrated and welcomed into the wonder of female power.

Rilla remembered the rapture she felt when the neume of a preborn found her. During that ritual, she was invited to join all the female minds in her circle as they shared the sacred knowledge about the creation of life. Age-old neumes of the joys and fears held close by females through generations were shared and passed onto the young females.

During the days of celebration, females honoured the new mother and her preborn, making promises to provide a community of wisdom and love for the new Abrax. Once the preborn's neumes quieted, the celebrations drew to a close and the mother's nest was prepared for the youngling's arrival.

Rilla was grateful to have the knowledge passed onto her from the older females during her rapture, but she was sad that she and her preborn would not be celebrated within a circle of females. Her little one would not neume with Neeva or her mother. No one would prepare Rilla's nest and promise to share their wisdom and love with her youngling.

The archive records about walker birthing were abundant. Rilla compared these records to the wisdom of the neumes shared during welcoming celebrations. She knew that Abrax babies developed and grew at the same rate as walker babies. She calculated that, any day now, the small halfling inside her would be ready to be born.

The baby was restless waiting in her tiny watery world. *Patience—love—joy*, Rilla neumed to her daughter.

Curiosity—frustration—wonder, was the reply.

Soon, my little one. Rilla was curious, too. She wondered what her daughter would look like. And she also worried for her.

Since Rilla's transformation, she had been challenged by bouts of illness that seemed to have no cause, and she had been so much sicker during the months when her daughter grew inside her. She was always thirsty, but when she drank water it never seemed to quench her thirst. She often felt ill and weak, and her head ached like it might crack open.

When Rilla felt unwell, she craved the sea. All she wanted was to float weightless in the warm shallows. The sickness and pain always faded when she could spend time in the sea.

She worried that her illness might have made the baby sick, but she would have known by now if something were wrong. She had learned during the nesting celebrations that the preborn exchanges neumes with its mother for two reasons: to build a bond, and to show that it's viable and ready for life in the sea.

At that moment, as if to reassure Rilla, her daughter flipped and frolicked, floating in her belly while Rilla floated in the shallow water. Her daughter was strong, but Rilla worried what her strong, restless daughter would look like. Where would this halfling baby belong, in the Above or in the Below?

Rilla decided she would have her baby alone. She would be the first to see the little one, just in case she didn't look as a walker babe should look.

Because she had felt it during the birthing celebrations in Lemuria, Rilla knew the youngling's signal indicating that the birth was near. When she felt her daughter's neumes go quiet, she readied herself for her arrival. Choosing a shallow sandy pool on the other side of the peninsula as her daughter's birthing nest, she secretly decorated it with shells and stones and coral.

It was dawn on her daughter's third quiet day. Rilla had left Marcus sleeping and was floating in the cool water of her nesting pool when she felt the beginnings of the birth pains.

'By the end of this day I'll have a daughter,' she whispered. *Welcome—love—joy.*

Curiosity—joy—love, came a faint neume in response.

Rilla didn't tell Marcus about the birth pains. She struggled through her few responsibilities around the station. Then she walked away for what everyone thought was her daily swimming session. She took herself around to her nesting pool, out of sight of the station.

She carefully spread the soft, blue cloth she had brought with her to wrap up the baby on the rocks to warm. She stepped over the ring of shells she had placed around the edge of the sheltered rock pool, sunk into the water that had been warmed during the day, and prepared to welcome her new halfling daughter into the world.

THE ABOVE

Trin stretched and looked around the cave; she could tell by the sinking patch of light low on the back wall that she had slept well past sunrise. Sharly was already up and out, and Trin hadn't heard a thing. Even though she had promised herself to forget what she thought she had seen a few nights ago, the images of Andy and Kayn persisted, so she had been keeping watch from the cave late at night.

Sharly hadn't said anything about what had happened that night, and Trin hadn't brought it up again either, but she had sat up and watched as Andy and Kayn walked the ledge at night, talking privately. She waited to see if they would shimmer and change, but they remained solid and ordinary looking. She had tried to reach out with her mind, feeling for the pressure she had felt, but there was nothing. She had wasted precious sleep with nothing to show for it but fatigue.

Mal and Sharly were waiting for her when she snaked down the cliff. Mal handed her a steaming pannikin of protein porridge, piled high with berries.

'I like your style,' Trin said. 'Thanks heaps.'

'Most of the team are acting like jealous frubes because we got picked to work with Andy and Kayn,' said Sharly around a mouthful of porridge. 'I thought you'd rather eat watching the water.'

'Good call, Sharls.' Trin blew her friend a kiss, leaned against the cliff and dug her spoon into the steaming gloop.

'Andy and Kayn said they'd meet us at the Funnel in ten,' said Mal.

'But we're supposed to be working at the other end of the station, then up the peninsula.' Trin prickled with fresh suspicion; suddenly her breakfast tasted sour.

'Maybe they just want to get wetskins from the shed,' suggested Sharly. 'We've got to get ours, anyway.'

'They never wear skins, well, I haven't seen them using them,' said Trin.

'I asked them about that,' said Mal. 'They said the water's much warmer here compared to the temperatures they're used to, so they don't need skins.'

'Right.' Trin said. 'And where is it exactly that they come from? Nakki Station isn't listed. I checked.'

'Nakki is new,' said Mal. 'Meg says she received a message through the net-stream. Well, she actually said Jasper got the message and passed it on. Anyway, she says they're solid.'

'Solid,' mumbled Trin, remembering when she'd seen them looking very unsolid.

The tide had fallen to half-low by the time Andy and Kayn had finished with the instructions for using the tagging equipment. The water in the Funnel was uncommonly flat. Trin watched it gently undulating, growing more restless with each lazy wave that rolled through. She drew in a breath to make a comment about being kept waiting and the drawn-out instructions, but Mal bristled and nudged her so she didn't. This was really important to Mal, and to her as well. If it would help her stay at the station to study, it was worth holding her tongue.

'We missed the high tide,' mumbled Mal.

'Maybe they'll stop talking by low tide.' Sharly tried to stifle a laugh.

'We have some swimming training for you do to next,' said Andy.

'We're all very experienced in the water,' Mal said.

'Yes, but we want to see how accomplished you are at manoeuvring under water,' said Kayn. 'Please attempt to dive and retrieve these objects when I ask you.' He dropped some weights into the water.

'I've only been swimming for about ... all my life,' whispered Trin.

'At least we're finally going to get wet,' Sharly whispered back as they got into the water.

They each took turns diving and retrieving things. With each retrieval they had to go a little deeper, which meant they spent longer holding their breath each time.

Andy and Kayn watched them closely. Whenever Mal and Sharly were out diving, and Trin was alone with Kayn and Andy, they fired questions at her.

'Can you tell me more about how you're able to locate the fish?' asked Andy.

'Can you sense them now?' asked Kayn.

'Cut back, I didn't say I could locate the fish. It's just a hunch I get,' stammered Trin. 'Like I said before, it's probably just luck.'

'How does this hunch feel?' asked Andy. 'Is it a sound?'

'When did this ability first start?' asked Kayn.

'It's not an ability, just a hunch, okay?' Trin was starting to get another hunch now, and it was telling her that this whole dive thing was dodgy. The rapid-fire questions of the near interrogation left her feeling confused and frustrated. 'Look, are we snorkelling today or not?' she blurted.

Mal and Sharly had resurfaced just in time to hear Trin's outburst. When she saw Mal cringe, Trin quickly added,

'I'd hate it if you missed the ebb at low tide, then you wouldn't get a chance to do any tagging.'

'Of course,' said Andy, flashing another of his looks at Kayn. 'Thank you for your concern.'

When they finally gathered the equipment and headed to the peninsula, Trin's mind felt murky and her head ached.

'Aren't you feeling well, Trin?' asked Andy.

'Yeah, you're looking a bit grey,' said Mal.

Sharly gave Trin a grim nod. 'Very pale,' she whispered.

Trin rubbed her face to try to stop it getting any paler.

'We've made you all work very hard so far with your training,' said Andy. 'We'll have a snack before we begin diving.'

Andy immediately brought out some single-serve flasks. 'It's hot chocolate,' he said.

Kayn held a box of something that looked like protein bars.

'I'll be fine,' said Trin, holding up her hand to refuse.

'I insist,' said Andy. 'It would be irresponsible of me to not properly prepare you for your tasks.'

Andy and Kayn glanced at each other, and Trin bristled. This time she was *sure* she'd felt something pass between them.

'It wouldn't hurt to take a quick break, Trin.' Mal looked at her pleadingly.

Trin didn't want to do anything that might affect their chances of selection for future projects, so she grumbled a little but took the flask Andy handed her, and forced herself to eat the offered snack.

The drink tasted odd, too sweet, but she knew she had no choice but to finish it. Her stomach felt queasy as they toted the gear up towards the peninsula, and for a moment she felt dizzy, but she wasn't going to say anything that might stop this project going ahead.

It was low tide now, and the usually submerged shelves of rock that ran the length of the peninsula were fully exposed. In some places pools had formed in the hollows, but mostly the plants and creatures that lived anchored to the rock lay unprotected, looking like a saggy, wilted garden. Clumps of pink sea plants, and the long threads of Neptune's beads, lay limp against the rocks. Spongy sea-fingers slumped over, waiting for the water to return and buoy them up once more. Among the wilting foliage, anemones and limpets sat anchored to the rock. They had sealed themselves up to wait out their time exposed to the hostility of the air.

Andy and Kayn stepped the equipment down to the lower ledge, and settled the floating table and gear into the water. Trin, Sharly and Mal clambered down behind them and pushed off into the sea.

During the afternoon they worked their way systematically along the edge of the shelf until they were near the point of the headland, at the Blender. The channel was slightly calmer now because it was low tide, but the current ripped through in its usual menacing way.

Trin took a moment to look across at Lighthouse Island and saw the rag flapping in the window. Her stomach clenched. The feeling of being watched was much stronger today. She shook the sensation away and forced herself to concentrate on the job.

Andy had Trin constantly seeking out tiny hiding places under the water and netting specimens for him. Then he glanced at them almost disinterestedly and handed them onto Kayn, who was working with Mal and Sharly to tag the struggling fish with microtrackers before releasing them again.

Trin opened her mind to the soft signals that moved between the fish. When fish found a morsel of food in a tight crevice and wanted to share it, they gave out fuddled location messages. Sometimes the fish signalled to warn each other of dangers lurking in the reef. Behind this constant chatter, Trin felt flashes of the same watching sensation that she had sensed before. She caught herself, more than once, surfacing and expecting to see someone watching her.

She surfaced now and looked across the Blender again, remembering how strongly she had felt that same watching presence when she had been on the island. She had felt the other signals, too, the ones that had assured her she was well and healthy. They had turned out be true, so perhaps someone *was* watching her, but who?

Her thoughts were interrupted by the float table banging into her shoulder.

Mal glared at her. 'They seem impressed with you, Trin.' It didn't sound much like a compliment. 'Do you want to do some tagging and I'll help Andy for a while?'

'Sure,' she said, and moved towards Kayn. 'Can I do some tagging now? I want to practise the technique you taught—'

'We'll be changing our strategy now,' interrupted Andy. 'Trin, you'll go on around to the other side of the headland with me to ... scout the area. Mal and Sharly, please catch fish for Kayn to tag. We'll all meet at the far side of the peninsula later.'

Trin felt a strange wave of concern and caution wash through her mind, but she ignored it.

'While I'm gone you can show Kayn how awesome you are,' she whispered to Mal.

'Crankin'.' Mal smiled, and he and Sharly waved as Trin followed Andy.

Kayn drifted along the ledge, looking for the next location. He glided face down in the water for what seemed to Mal an impressively long time without needing a breath before finally stopping near a half-submerged thicket of kelp. 'We'll collect specimens here.'

'I think this weed will be a problem,' said Mal.

'The weed's not a problem for me,' Kayn said. 'Mal, Sharly, can you please get the tags ready? I can see some specimens below.' He pushed away from them into deeper water.

'How can we see anything with all this weed here?' Mal asked.

'Cut back, Mal,' Sharly mumbled. 'He knows what he wants.'

'Is there a problem?' Kayn was looking back at them, stony faced.

'No,' said Mal, as Kayn continued to drift further out. 'I just thought I was doing the diving now ... ouch.' Mal rubbed his head.

Kayn turned without speaking again and duck-dived under the water.

'Are you okay?' Sharly said to Mal.

'Yeah, bit of a brain ache, that's all.'

'We'll have to stop soon anyway. When the tide's high it'll get too rough.' Sharly pulled the floating workbench closer and started to reload the tag guns. 'If you're wiped out, you can head back and I'll finish tagging,'

'Nah, I'll be fine, the pain's fading now.' Mal rubbed his temples.

'What was that?' said Sharly.

'What?'

'Something brushed around my ankles.'

'Did it sting you?' asked Mal urgently.

'No, it just felt creepy, but it's gone now.' She turned back to the table.

'Not gone, Sharls ... it's over here now. Quimby, it feels slimy.' Mal looked down into the water. 'I can't see anything.'

'You catch it, I'll tag it,' joked Sharly.

'No problem.'

'Hey, shouldn't Kayn be back by now?' asked Sharly. 'I thought he was supposed to be bringing more samples.'

'I'll swim out and have a look.' Mal moved to glide out to where he had seen Kayn dive down. He felt something again. This time it didn't brush past; he felt it wrapping itself around one leg, then both legs. 'My feet are tangled in something, I'm snagged,' he called, as the tangle took firmer hold of his legs.

'I'll take a look,' said Sharly. She glided out towards Mal. 'What! I'm stuck, too.'

Whatever was holding Sharly resisted all her efforts to twist her ankles free. She tried to swim away from the rocks. Using all the strength she had, she clawed at the water and kicked hard to shake herself free, but whatever it was had started twining itself around her calves. She could feel its feathery touch around her knees. It was gripping her legs tightly and she felt it pulling her down into the water.

'Mal!' she cried out, stretching a hand towards him.

He flung his hand out to meet hers, but as he drew closer he disappeared under the water, leaving a swirl of turbulence as he sank away. A trail of bubbles was the only sign that he was down there, somewhere.

Sharly kicked furiously at the tightening bonds, but the more she did so the tighter they became. She strained to comprehend this unknown thing. It felt like some kind of sea plant, but it moved like an eel, wrapping itself

216

further up her legs and around her hips. Whatever it was, it suddenly jerked her under the water. She clawed back up to the surface, gulped a breath and screamed.

She felt the plant-eel thing coiling higher up her body. Wrapping around her, it pressed her arms against her body and squeezed. Then she was submerged again, and being tugged backwards through the water towards the partially submerged reef.

Jagged rocks pressed into her back. The thing released its grip on her arms, but she remained frozen, scared that the bonds might tighten again if she moved. The slithering tendrils remained tightly wrapped around her lower body. Only her head was above the lapping water.

'Mal!' Sharly stared out across the water, searching for any sign of Mal or Kayn. She took shallow, panicky breaths. Black splotches of dizziness were strobing her vision. She saw movement, a wake trail. Something was moving towards her, fast.

Mal was slammed up against the rock next to her. He lifted his head above the water and snatched rasping gulps of air. 'Sharly!' he gasped.

'I'm here,' she sobbed. 'Are you okay?'

Mal just stared at her, wide eyed.

'What's going on down there?' she asked. 'What are these things?'

The answer to Sharly's question appeared in the water in front of them. Several dark fronds, like flattened-out eels, squirmed up until they were just beneath the surface. They roiled in the water between Sharly and Mal. Then, five leathery tendrils rose out of the water, standing erect and leaning close to Mal. The dark, weedy blades weaved back and forth for a long moment.

'Burley!' gasped Mal. 'No way!'

Sharly watched him, frantically trying to move away from the weed. Mal's eyes blinked wildly. 'Mal, what's going on?' she demanded.

At the sound of her voice, the black blades turned, and Sharly was confronted by the unfathomable strangeness of five pairs of eyes blinking at her out of five impossible faces. Her heart slammed in her chest and her throat tightened.

The eyes blinked disrhythmically, once, and again, and then the faces submerged.

'What was *that*?' she squeaked.

'I don't think I want to know,' said Mal. 'Do you think Kayn's all right?.'

Sharly thought of the rippling, watery images of Kayn and Andy she had teased Trin about. 'My guess is he's more all right than we are,' she said.

'What does that mean?' Mal took in a mouthful of water and coughed. He looked up at the rocks, to where a trail of dried flotsam indicated the high-water mark. The tide was coming in, and they were both being held below the high-water line.

Sharly followed his gaze. They looked at each other. Mal nodded.

They both began to struggle against their inhuman bonds.

THE BETWEEN

Happy birthday to you. Hip-hip …'

'Hooray!'

'Hip-hip …'

'Hooray!'

'Hip-hip …'

'Hooray!'

'You must be so proud,' said Meg, hugging Rilla and Marcus. 'She's so clever and strong. Walking everywhere, and even swimming.'

'She's wonderful.' Marcus smiled broadly at his daughter. 'Aren't you, Little Fish?' He kissed her on the forehead.

'Barpy barpday,' his daughter said, and squirmed from his arms to play with her toys.

'You know, you two really have started something,' said Meg. 'Now lots of the others are deciding to move their families to the station. They see that you two trust the storm shields to keep your family safe, and High and Dry is so far away. It's hard on partners and the grommets.'

'Grommets?' said Marcus.

'Jasper's word not mine, but I like it. Grommets. Kids. Anyway, I've got plenty of extra work, organising lessons through the school link on the stream, for those kids that are old enough for lessons. It's a good kind of busy, though. I like what the families bring to the station. It feels less like an outpost and more like we're making progress and creating something important here.' Meg wrapped Rilla and Marcus in another quick hug.

'I'd be happy to help you with the school link,' said Rilla, knowing it would give her an added opportunity to learn about the wider world of the Above.

'Thanks, Rilla, I'm sure I'll need some help when more grommets arrive, but I don't want you taking on too much. How have you been feeling since your last checkup?'

'Good ... about the same.'

Rilla thought that the strange sickness had only worsened because she'd been pregnant, but it had continued and become much more debilitating in the year following the birth. She was often weak, and always felt as though she was on the edge of sleep. Her head ached, and she got confused and frustrated easily.

Meg was kind, and Rilla knew she was concerned for her wellbeing, but the checkups were very difficult. During those sessions, with Meg so close and examining her even more closely, Rilla needed to neume very strongly to hide the things about her that would always remain Abrax. Her shrivelled gills and the flimsy ruffles of skin that remained between her toes where her fins had fallen away. The soft, weak joints of her knees and ankles. The iridescent flicker in her irises.

Rilla always had to neume to alter people's perceptions about her. But now she also had to send out even stronger neumes that would hide the decline she was suffering, and this mental effort took so much energy that it weakened her even further.

Rilla thought about when she was young, and the way Lana had constantly neumed to Rilla about the catalyst failing, trying to make Rilla too scared to even consider ascending.

The Gathering of Colours have records, Lana had neumed to her so long ago. *They're held in secret, but I know an apprentice in the record chamber. He neumed with me.* Lana eyes had sparkled with mischief and pride. *The records neumed that once they'd found a dead monster sinking into the darkening sea, half Abrax, half walker.*

Only one? Rilla had neumed, disregarding the cautionary tale.

She remembered that in the Deeps, when she had asked to take the catalyst, Pelagya had warned her that it could fail. She had neumed of the risks, and again Rilla had pushed the idea away.

But now she was struggling to conceal the throbbing pain in her head, and her itchy dry mouth. She had started to think more realistically about how many more Abrax might have chosen ascension and failed the transformation, never to be found. Those failed, half-formed creatures would have been weak. They would have been eaten by one danger animal or another as their lifeless bodies drifted back down to the Below.

Even though Rilla hadn't shared their fate on her changing day, she wasn't sure what would become of her. These days she needed to spend more and more time in the sea to keep her illness at bay.

Her knowledge of the oceans, and the scientific expertise she had gained at the station were causing her to draw frightening conclusions. One of the station projects involved studying the fish that became ill with bloat because the salinity levels in the sea had lowered. The fish were sick because they were exposed to too much fresh water. Rilla compared this to her own symptoms, so similar to bloat. Could it be that she was becoming sick because of exposure to too much fresh water?

Rilla sat alone on the headland, staring out across the water. The throbbing in her head was insignificant in comparison to the ache growing in her heart as she accepted that her time as a walker would surely need to be over soon. It was unbearable to think about, because it meant that her time with Marcus and her precious Little Fish would also have to end.

How could she leave Marcus and their daughter? Sobs rose in her like a storm.

If she were to stay alive, it would mean returning to the sea to get away from the fresh water that was poisoning her. She couldn't remain in the Above and survive. But she could never return to Lemuria, or to the kind and wise Pelagya in the Deeps because her gills were shrivelled and stunted. Her only hope was to find a place to dwell somewhere in the Between and watch the life she could no longer be a part of.

THE ABOVE

You have slowed,' said Andy over his shoulder, as they swam along the southern side of the peninsula. 'I feel hot,' Trin said.

Andy nodded and stared at her for a moment. 'It's the exertion,' he said, then turned and swam away.

'Frube,' Trin mumbled. 'Thanks for the sympathy.' She loosened the neck of her wetskin and followed him.

The heat continued to increase. Trin thought of the fish her father cooked in his pan over the fire. She imagined herself frying. It felt like her sweat was simmering on her skin inside the suit. She'd been swimming hard, following Andy's orders and manoeuvring in and out of tight spaces in the rocks to net the fish. Every time she got a chance, she tugged at the neck and arms of her wetskin to let some cooler water seep in, but she still felt hot.

It was hardly possible, but she was getting hotter. The wetskin felt like it was getting tighter. She badly wanted to be free of its stifling constriction. Then she realised that the sea was calmer today, and she didn't need to worry about being scuffed on the rocks. She started to unzip her wetskin.

Then she hesitated. Inside her head there was an echoing, heard-felt message: *Caution—home*. She ignored it as another wave of heat surged across her body.

She pulled back the wetskin like a rubber banana peel. Pulling her arms free, she pushed the suit down her body and over her hips. The cool water swirled around her, giving momentary relief. She yanked the skin free from its last grip around her legs and flung it onto the rocks above the high-tide line. She would collect on the way back.

The currents—cool, warm, cool again—ribboned across Trin's skin. She paddled back and forth, chasing the coolest currents, holding herself in each one, feeling the relief of chilly water on her skin, but each time she felt the heat building again.

'Did you see that?' asked Andy, sounding excited. He didn't mention her jettisoned wetskin.

'Sorry, no, what did I miss?'

'A large blue-bone, I'm sure that's what it was. I've never known of one to be found in this area.'

'And you won't. We've never had one in the nets, ever, so you were probably mistaken.'

'Well, we have a little time before the others catch up to us. Shall we dive down and take a look? I think you'll be surprised with what you discover during this dive.'

Caution—home. Again, Trin ignored the echo. She could only think about the heat. Maybe, if she dived deeper, she would swim through an extra-cold current and finally cool herself off properly.

She shrugged and nodded to Andy. 'Which way?'

'Follow me,' he said, duck-diving under the surface. *Not Below.*

Trin took a breath and followed. She was down about two metres when she realised that she had lost sight of Andy. She did some rapid circles, searching through the blue to locate him. As she did, her mask and snorkel slipped off her face. She groped around for them, unsuccessfully, and started to kick upwards to head for the surface but something stopped her. Something was pulling her down. She looked down to see what had snagged her and locked eyes with Andy ... blue Andy. He was holding her leg and pulling her into deeper water.

Trin kicked out, pulling to get loose of his grip. She stared into his haunting, blue, mask-less face and shook her head in a violent gesture. *No!*

His grip on her leg didn't loosen, just relocated slightly. His other hand gripped her arm as he released her leg. His face was level with hers now, and he was staring at her in the same studious way that he observed the fish they collected for tagging.

Trin thrashed and kicked to free herself so she could get to the surface. Her ears filled with the panicked thumping of her heart, and the echoes of the screams and sobs that were trapped in her throat. She looked up at the glassy surface and the air above, and let fly with more thrashing kicks.

Andy continued to pull her deeper. They descended, away from the rock ledge and towards the darker sandy slopes. Trin's throat burned, and she felt the spasms as her lungs pleaded to inhale. She pressed her lips together and fought the urge building in her to suck the saltwater into her body. The muscles of her neck and chest burned with the need to breathe. Time seemed to slow and distort around her. The panicked seconds stretched out.

Though she knew the water at this depth should be much cooler, the heat on her skin remained and was intensifying. Now the skin at the base of her throat burned, as though she had been scalded. She thought she must have been stung by some floating creature. What else could be the cause of such intense burning?

Taking one hand away from the job of punching Andy, she touched her face and neck, feeling for stinger tentacles, but there was nothing. Maybe she'd swallowed a small jellyfish when she lost her mask. That would explain the burning pain in her throat and in her chest.

She ran her fingertips across the usually smooth skin that covered her collarbones. There were raised mounds of swelling running from both sides of her neck and out to each shoulder. Along the centre of each mound, she felt hot, angry ridges of flesh. They stung in the saltwater as though she had been cut.

Andy stopped for a moment and turned to watch as Trin investigated the rising welts. Through her clouding, panicked vision, she thought she saw a satisfied smile flow across Andy's blue face. She swung another angry punch in the direction of the blue smile and strained to pull her arm free. Andy's grip tightened.

They could only have been descending for seconds, maybe a minute. The water was growing darker all around now. Trin twisted to look up at the glinting of the sunlight on the surface that was now far above her. Her mind buzzed as it used the last of her oxygen.

With her remaining strength, she dug her nails into the flesh on Andy's arms and kicked out at his legs. She struck as hard as she could, and as she made contact she flexed her toes to gouge at the skin of his legs. Her feet slid across his skin, almost as though it was slimy, slick, somehow. Then she felt a strong, coiling limb wrap around her legs, constricting them so she could no longer kick out. She wanted to sob, scream.

Help—help me please.

Andy's blue, shiny face stared at her. He now looked exactly as he had appeared on the evening he had arrived, when she'd seen him in the dining hall, just before she'd passed out. She looked down, or was it up, to see what had trapped her legs. She saw a blue torso, with the strange skirt of dreadlocks, and beyond that, more pearly-blue skin. One leathery leg was wrapped around both of hers. The other leg was no longer a leg. Instead of a foot, it ended in a shiny, translucent fin. That fin was powering them down deep into the water.

Trin reeled at the sight and took in a harsh, burning breath. Waves of pain scorched through her chest. She stiffened and waited for the end. Her lungs spasmed again, then again, then calmed. She felt the rise and fall of her chest, the movement of breathing, but that couldn't be happening.

In her confused euphoria she joked with herself. No surprise that I'd think heaven would look like the deep ocean. But why hadn't she noticed the moment she died? Maybe that's what drowning was like.

A strong message echoed inside her mind: *Not dead, changed.*

Twisting around wildly, she tried to see where ... who ... the message had come from. She looked at Andy. He only stared at her, still looking self-satisfied, as though he was examining a fish specimen. He turned away and continued to pull her down deeper into the darkening waters.

Trin's mind convulsed. *Scared—confused—no more—no more—dead.*

A calming message filled her mind, a strong flood of thoughts and feelings. *Not dead—changed—new—gulp—breathe.*

Though it couldn't be happening, Trin could feel her lungs expanding, breathing. But how?

Changed—wonderful—soon safe—soon free—loved—soon—believe. The message faded and Trin continued to descend into the darkness, trapped in Andy's grip.

THE BETWEEN

Today there was another birthday cake, and now the station had grown. There were many children for her daughter to play with and to sing 'Happy Birthday' as she blew out her candles. Rilla needed to attend this birthday party in a wheelchair; she had become frailer and today she was weaker than usual.

Worried, Marcus wondered how long they would have together. He was sure that moving closer to medical attention would prevent Rilla getting sicker. He had started to talk about them moving to New Sydney, where Rilla could have specialists to treat her.

Rilla knew with certainty that she would die if she moved away from the sea. She could not let this happen. And what of her daughter? How much did her daughter need the sea? The child always fussed terribly when they missed a day of swimming because of a storm. Rilla had shared the youngling's neumes; she knew how the sea enchanted and soothed her Little Fish. Though there were no physical signs of the Abrax half appearing in her daughter, Rilla couldn't risk what the move away from the sea might do to her.

Rilla relished every moment she had with her daughter and husband. She knew they had very little time left together, and she wanted to fill her heart to bursting with loving memories that would sustain her after she returned to the sea.

Maybe returning to the sea wouldn't stop her getting sicker and she would die anyway. What she hoped with all her heart was that she would somehow find a way to heal herself and be able to reunite with her precious family. She had to believe there was hope. It was the only thing that would give her the strength and courage to leave and return to the sea.

One cool autumn afternoon, when she was swimming and Marcus and Little Fish were exploring the rockpools, Rilla happened upon a dead dugong. It had washed up in the shallows, and lay tattered and bloated at the water's edge. She knew this was her opportunity to start the next and saddest chapter of her life.

Using all her strength, she pushed the creature up onto a small sheltered ledge at the end of the peninsula near where she had been swimming. She knew Marcus would walk past it when he was returning home. Then she swam across the channel and hid herself on the island that had been her first home. She watched as the two people she loved most, in both the worlds she had known, walked together along the narrow gritty beach. She felt sorrow at being the cause of the sadness that was to come

As Marcus and Little Fish drew closer to the place where the dugong lay, Rilla neumed *Soothe—blue— loved—doze* to lull her daughter to sleep and spare her any memories of the immeasurable sadness this day would bring. She saw Marcus lift his daughter into his arms. She saw her Little Fish nod her head down on her father's shoulder. In moments she was asleep.

Now Rilla put all her failing energy into conjuring the neumed images that would transform the dead dugong into the illusion that it was her dead body lying on the gritty sand. These neumes were her strongest. Like all her previous neumes had been, these would be accepted and kept just as any other memory was kept.

Marcus and the others at the station would all believe the dugong was Rilla's body. Her neumes would make them think she had finally been overwhelmed by her mysterious illness, and weakened so much that she had drowned and washed up on the headland. She had felt the neumes of concern and the expectation of her death from many people at the station, so she knew that a detailed examination of the body was unlikely. Her neumes would make sure of that.

From her hiding place she saw Marcus approaching the headland, his arms full of their sleeping daughter wrapped in his shirt. She pushed all her strength and effort into a neume that made the dead dugong appear to look like her. As she did, Marcus lifted his gaze and stared directly at the dead imposter. He quaked and fumbled with the sleeping bundle, then caught himself before she fell. The child startled and whimpered.

Soothe—blue—doze.

She wriggled in her father's arms and remained asleep.

Marcus ran to where the imposter lay and hastily placed his daughter down on the gritty sand. He knelt and scooped Rilla's false body into his arms. *Shock—anguish—anger—black—red—black.*

Rilla was almost drowned in the wave of his grief.

Marcus rocked and sobbed, holding his false wife.

Rilla watched and sobbed with him. She wrapped her arms around herself to squeeze down on her own pain, and she rocked in time with him as though she was lying there in his arms instead of the dugong corpse.

The sun dropped low in the sky. A silhouette—Jasper—approached in the fading light.

Rilla wanted to cross back to the peninsula, to change her neumes and somehow take back her false

234

perceptions, and make it all fade away so she could be with them again. She gripped the jagged rock she was hiding behind until her palms burned, bled. Breathing heavily with the effort, she redoubled the strength of her neume. She would ensure that everyone would see Jasper carrying the child, and Marcus carrying a dead Rilla, along the rock shelf and back to the station.

The dead creature was buried and mourned in Rilla's place. She didn't sleep or eat for the three days it took to arrange her funeral and bury her at the top of the cliffs. They planted a tree on her grave. One day the body they believed to be Rilla's would nourish the soil. In a few seasons, a tree would bear sweet fruit and they would remember her fondly at harvest time.

Rilla's heart broke daily as she watched her beloved husband grieve, and she felt the neumes of confusion when her daughter asked, 'Where has Mummy gone?' Rilla listened to her daughter's cries, carried on the salty evening breezes. She softly crooned the song that had comforted her since she was so very small.

Calm—loved—protected, she neumed across the water and through evening darkness. *I love you*, she sang into her daughter's mind, *more than all the little pearly shells.*

Through the years, her daughter thrived and grew. Rilla returned from hiding when she could, to watch from her lonely place between worlds. Her only joy was the neumes her daughter unknowingly sang out and shared with her.

THE ABOVE

The dark, flattened faces with their arrhythmic, blinking eyes had dropped below the water, but they had not released their captives. Sharly and Mal twisted and pulled to get free of the monstrous weed creatures, but this only caused their captors to tighten their grip further.

It was almost high tide, and the rising water was lapping around their chins. When the swell lifted, the waves smacked into their faces. They spluttered and spat, trying to clear their throats and catch a precious breath before the next wave rolled in. They both knew they could never stretch enough to remain above water at high tide.

'Stretching our necks will only work for a few more minutes,' coughed Mal.

'Here comes another one,' said Sharly.

She braced herself, clamping her mouth shut, trying to extend her neck and raise her face above the water. She gasped as the wave smacked into her face and flowed past. Then she noticed that when she held herself still, bracing for a wave, the weed-creature relaxed its grip, just a fraction. As soon as she started trying to get loose again, the squirming weed-creatures would constrict painfully around her legs and body once more.

She reached her one free hand out towards Mal. He gripped it and coughed violently as the next wave flowed into his mouth.

'Mal, have you noticed these things keep loosening their grip when we keep still?'

'Yeah.' Mal spat and strained his neck further to stay above the water.

'How about we try a shubee?'

'Fake it how?' he asked.

'These things want us dead,' she spluttered. 'So if we go limp, act dead—'

'They might release us.'

Sharly kept hold of Mal's hand. She relaxed and tried to calm her breathing, taking tiny breaths so her lungs barely expanded. She faked random buoyancy, tilting and partially submerging as each wave knocked into her. The weed-creatures loosened their grip slightly.

She held her breath totally now, and let herself sink under the water. She thought of the game she and Trin used to play when they were young, floating in the rockpools, pretending they lived in the sea and could stay underwater forever. They would stare at each other and smile goofy, rippling smiles until they both burst out of the water gasping and laughing.

The weed-creatures fully relaxed their grip. She could feel herself bobbing in the loose coils of weed that now floated freely around her. She waited, hungry for a breath.

Still—safe now.

Sharly stiffened, her blood turned icy. The words in her head were not hers. Her heart hammered. Cut back! She fumbled to find her footing on the rocks. She had been about to surface and bolt, hopefully clear of the weird weed-creatures, but she felt compelled to stay.

Still—peace—float—safe now—free soon.

An overwhelming calm warmness washed away Sharly's panic. She felt as though she was in a bubble. Everything went still; time stopped. She was surrounded by a circular swirl. A whirlpool was somehow forming. Something brushed past her. She heard the beginnings of her own cries in her ears, but they didn't grow. She could not cry out. She thought this should bother her, but for now the calmness was everywhere.

Torpid —no purpose—unconjure.

These thoughts were not for Sharly. She realised, somehow, that they were for the weed-creatures.

Spasms rippled through the loosened coils of weed that was floating around Sharly's legs. She stiffened, pulling her face from the water and gasping. The weed-creatures went suddenly rigid, floating like driftwood.

She turned, looking for Mal, and saw he was staring back at her. 'Did you hear that?' she asked.

'Well ... I ... there was something,' he said between puffed breaths.

'Can you get loose?' Sharly pushed against the rigid basket of weedy tentacles and floated out of the tangle. She bumped into them and braced for them to constrict around her again, but they just twisted and bobbed on the surface with their dead eyes staring at her.

She heaved herself up out of the water and onto the sharp rocks. Wedging her feet into a crevice, she braced herself and leaned over to help Mal as he scrambled out. They sat, breathing heavily, and watched as the flat leathery tendrils floated and turned over in the lapping waves like dead fish floating on the surface.

'Look at their eyes.' Sharly shivered and pointed to the lifeless grey globs on the ghoulish, dead faces. 'What mutant horror was that? And what killed them?'

'Pull your feet up,' said Mal, pointing at the whirlpool current. 'Whatever it is, it's still down there.'

They watched as a long shimmering shadow rippled below the surface, then the shadow turned and headed out to sea. As it disappeared, they saw a fin ... two fins ... at the end of a fast-moving pearl-blue shape.

'Cowabunga,' rasped Mal.

'Trin and I saw something like that before,' Sharly said, 'but we thought we were just imagining—' She grabbed Mal. 'Trin! We've got to find her.' Sharly jumped up and started running.

Mal caught up with her as she rounded the peninsula. They stopped at the crumpled pile of Trin's wetskin lying on the rocks.

Home—people—help.

The non-voice blasted into their heads until they stopped and doubled over from the pain. They wanted to keep running, to find Trin but the compulsion to turn for home was overwhelming.

Home.

Sharly picked up Trin's wetskin, and she and Mal turned and ran for the station.

THE BELOW

The pain had faded from Trin's throat and chest, and somehow she wasn't dead. But she was still being pulled further and further from the shore, the station, and everyone she knew who kept her safe. But why? The blue arms and tentacle legs were still gripping her like a coiled vice. Her ears were filled with a bubbling, rushing tumult as they raced through the water. They had slowed their descent, and now they sped along the edge of a drop-off, at the top of an underwater cliff. Below her was the darkness of deeper water.

Milkshake in a blender, she heard her shocked brain say, describing the storm of bubbles all around her as they speed through the water. She strained to see where she was, and which way they were travelling, hoping she could turn and resurface if she could get free. Maybe she could fight this ... thing that used to be Andy, surprise it.

As she thought about how she might overwhelm her lone blue kidnapper, she felt another set of hands grip her. She turned to see a blue version of Kayn's face. She jolted. She had been horribly right about these two ... men. Her mind fizzed as she tried to make sense of these strange-within-strange happenings.

How am I here? *Why* am I here? These were thoughts she could not voice without air to talk. But she could breathe-gulp. She felt the cool water move down her throat, then there was some strange internal effervescence and the water exited, warmed by her body, through the amazing feathery slits that had opened near her collarbones.

Gills—gulp—be brave—safe soon. The chain of ideas came to her from that same somewhere she had sensed before. Soothing feelings came with the ideas. As they washed over her, she calmed.

The darkening blue world was opening out in front of her. Beyond the edge of the drop-off she could see nothing but a blue-black infinity. Though she knew she should be trying to free herself, she had become distracted and curious. She stared at the scene that lay below and in front of her.

Lying randomly all along the slope were things that remained from before the rising. She could see tilted houses, buckled and pushed over by the constant movement of the currents. They were now only mounds of wrecked and rotting driftwood that could not float away because they were held down where they had crumpled by the weight of their roofs. Rows of these rubble piles that used to be houses were arranged in straight lines, along what Trin recognised used to be roads. The sandy earth that had been under these strips of road had long ago been washed away by the constant waves, and now the roads were buckled black ribbon decorated with seagrass that had sprouted in the cracks.

A spaghetti junction of old traffic lights, twisted by the endless passing waves, crouched where two old roads met. Signs, directing the way to this shop or that cafe, were now partially hidden behind shields of barnacles.

An oversized smiling head that used to show the entrance to a beachside amusement park was lying in the sandy silt, with fish swimming in and out of its broken-toothed smile. An octopus flowed from one of its hollow eyes and scuttled across its cheek, disappearing into a barnacled nostril.

Snot, thought Trin's overloaded brain. Then she felt a presence. Shark!

Kayne and Andy loosened their grip on her arms for just a second. Although she knew her captors were no longer the men she had known, she still thought of them by their names. She realised they must have felt it, too, because they stalled for a moment and looked around for a hiding place among the leftovers of the old flooded beach town.

Trin scanned for a safe place, too, but she could see nothing big enough to hide behind unless they split up, and she knew they weren't going to let her go. They tightened their grip and rushed on, away from the vibe of the approaching shark.

More sharks! Trin could feel two or three now, and they were circling, taking their time and stalking their prey, as though the three of them were a school of fish. Trin could feel the *hungry—anger* pulsing through the water and into her brain. She also felt her captors' grip on her arms faltering.

Kayn and Andy looked around nervously, trying to see where the sharks were coming from. They twisted and turned in the water, looking frantically into the murky distance. The never-ending blue devoured the light. The sharks were concealed perfectly somewhere in the blue blindness.

Trin's frustration came like a storm surge. If I'm going to have to face sharks, she thought, then I'll do it on my own. With a huge effort, she twisted and flicked free from blue Kayn and blue Andy and moved in the direction she knew they wouldn't follow. She swam *towards* where she felt the sharks.

Kayn and Andy made fitful grasps in her direction, but didn't come closer. They floated with their tails coiling and uncoiling. They looked at her, then into the blue behind her, scanning the water for the sharks. Then they froze and darted away.

Trin saw it then, a small one. It came from a different direction than the signals she had felt, but it was heading straight for her. She froze. She looked into the dark eyes of the half-thinking shark. She watched the halo of bubbles that formed as the creature sped through the water. She couldn't move. She watched as trails of bubbles slid down the length of the shark.

It turned. Its tail slapped her as it passed and spun her around.

She saw Kayn and Andy in the murky distance. They were no longer swimming. They had stopped, and she saw a trail of red. Then the blue distance swallowed them. The blood would attract the other sharks. This was her chance.

She disregarded the poor visibility and concentrated on feeling the sharks, on drawing the sharks to those blue goons. She tried to keep a mental lock on Kayn and Andy, and reached out to compel the sharks to follow them. Then doubt, and reality, swept back in. How come she wasn't dead yet? It didn't matter, she would be soon, unless she … Signal? She concentrated on the angry signals, and tried to conjure the illusion of a school of fish, making them appear to be some distance away from her and closer to the plume of blood.

The sharks were close now and moving fast. They would burst out of the blue gloom any second, and if her illusion failed they would attack her before she had time to realise she had failed. At least it would be a quick death.

In the blue distance, she could finally see the tiny trace of bubbles that must be a shark. The veil of bubbles surrounded the creature as it sped through the water. The water pulsed with the shark's primitive thoughts. *Anger—hunger—anger.* It was close now, so close. It was right in front of her. It wasn't turning away to follow her invented school of fish. Her illusion had failed. Trin imagined the shark stretching its jaws open, and she braced herself for the moment it would slam into her, slicing her with its razor teeth.

Nothing.

Something collided with her. It wrapped around her, scooping her up. Now she was speeding along inside a cocoon of bubbles. The bubbles fractured and re-formed, making clustered spheres of rainbow against the blue. The shades of blue around her were lightening. She must be rising. She could no longer feel the *angry—hungry* of the sharks. They must have changed course. What was happening?

The water was getting much lighter now. The harder she tried to think, the less sense it all made. Her brain finally let itself change gears and idle down, and like an outboard motor on a dingy, her brain spluttered and faltered. She lay inside the cocoon of bubbles as it sped through the blue. She looked up at the amazing jewels that were formed by sunlight hitting the water. They looked like liquid silver scales of light, floating on the surface.

Crankin'! I get to see this as I die.

Not dead, Little Fish. Changed—wonderful—loved, came a loud, clear echo.

Trin became fully alert again.

THE BETWEEN

Rilla had practised for many years and her neumes were strong, complete and always convincing, compelling. They had to be or she would never have been able to keep the secrets of her true nature during her life as a walker, or to stay hidden after her contrived death. Now she had constructed a third death for herself. The first had been neumed by Pelagya, the second was to save her life, and the third was to save her daughter.

Rilla had always thought that Lana's hate-filled obsessions might bring her sister to the surface, and she was right, Lana did come, but she never found Rilla.

When Trin's loud, uncontrolled neumes had blurted through the water Lana had felt them. Lana knew who Trin was, and she decided that if she couldn't bring Rilla back to the Below to gain twisted honour with her father, then Trin would be her prize.

Lana had gained control over Andy and Kayn, and sent them to do her hate-filled bidding.

Rilla would never have been discovered, but for the sake of her daughter she had been forced to take action.

First, she had neumed that she was alive and hidden in the Between, knowing Lana would now have two targets for her hatred. Rilla knew her sister couldn't resist coming closer, so she wouldn't miss the tragic scene Rilla had planned for her.

When Lana's two nakki, otherwise known as Kayn and Andy, had taken Trin, Rilla had conjured her strongest illusion. It showed Rilla racing to save her daughter from the attacking sharks. The nakki would see that mother and daughter were united, together in each other's arms as the sharks bore down on them, and in a frenzy of bubbling blood, their tragic lives would be over.

Now that she and Trin were believed to be dead, Rilla had sent the smaller shark toward Kayn and Andy. It had not killed them, but she had neumed with the shark and shared the smell of Abrax blood, the taste of flesh. Then she had sensed the two scared nakki lurking in their hiding place, watching as their blood clouded the water. Lana would not doubt the shark attack was real, with her nakki puppets injured.

It had been successful. Lana had neumed strongly, gloating and fizzing with satisfaction as she witnessed the final undoing of Rilla and her wretched halfling daughter. Lana and her two nakki had watched Rilla's illusion of the trailing ribbons of blood melt into the water as the sharks powered off into the depths to outrun the others in the hunting shiver, and avoid having their precious food stolen.

Now, Rilla knew, Lana and her two nakki would scuttle back to Lemuria, satisfied that no other younglings surfacing as part of the choosing would see Rilla or Trin and discover that Abrax had successfully ascended and made a life in the Above. Then the Gathering of Colours could continue to lie and make the Abrax believe there would never be a future where the walkers and the Abrax could come together.

Rilla locked her mind up tightly as she retreated into the blue. As they descended, she cast a strong bubble around Trin's muttering neumes to contain them, as she had often done with her own thoughts to keep them from Lana's reach.

As Rilla swam, cradling her daughter in her arms, she wondered what had spurred Lana on. What had convinced her to come to the Above? Had Lana persuaded Pelagya to break her secret and reveal that Rilla was alive? She thought of Pelagya's daughter,

Pontia. No one knew more than Rilla how much a mother would sacrifice to keep her child safe. Perhaps Lana had used Pontia against Pelagya somehow. But that had been years ago. Perhaps now it was Pontia who was held in the Deeps, forced to collude for the sake of her own daughter. Rilla realised that the hate and fear that the Gathering of Colours held must run as deep as the ocean.

In the darkening distance below, Rilla could see the two cowards glowing on either side of Lana as the three raced down, returning home. She had felt the neumes; the nakki thought they were heroes for the Abrax. They expected to return to Lemuria as champions of the Gathering of Colours. But Rilla had felt their true fate in Lana's neume, and it wasn't to be heroes.

Lana had used siren magic, the most powerful of the Abrax mind songs, to control the nakki. Choosing the way of the siren was the greatest wrong an Abrax could commit. Controlling fish or walkers was one thing, but controlling Abrax, even to do the bidding of the Gathering of Colours, was forbidden.

The twin secrets of Thal's meddling and Lana's siren magic would have to stay secret forever. Thal would never let the nakki return to Lemuria. Their fate was to be planted. They would not be Abrax for much longer. Soon they would be planted among the other hissi-weed, to turn into mindless leathery monstrosities and dwell in the Deeps forever. The fate of the hissi-weed in Pelagya's garden of horrors was for those Abrax who had strayed in their thinking or failed at a task. Their punishment was to be given a very different catalyst, which rooted them in place and diminished their minds. The hissi-weed garden was the perfect place to keep secrets.

Watching Trin, who lay limp in her arms, Rilla shuddered. Lana would surely have planted Trin down in the Deeps as well. Rilla had to ensure that she was strong enough to conceal and protect her daughter until Trin could learn to protect herself.

THE BETWEEN

Everything was spinning. Trin's head pounded and the horizon tilted as she tried to focus and make sense of everything. She could feel strong arms wrapped around her waist from behind as she was pulled up onto the slope of a gritty beach. From the corner of her blurry vision, she managed to see the very top of the lighthouse, but this view of it wasn't the side she usually saw from the station. Whoever had brought her here had come ashore on the far side of the island. They were totally out of sight of anyone who might be looking for Trin, or could help her.

Please be looking for me, she thought. Trin breathed hard, thinking of Kayn and Andy, then of the strong arms pulling her from the water. She looked down. Not blue.

Safe—loved—calm—safe.

Trin's mind unclenched slightly, but the questions flowed. What was happening? Why wasn't she dead? She tensed again as she recalled the horrible, frightening capture—the blue arms holding her, dragging her under water; her lungs bursting as she was pulled deeper and deeper; the cold wetness that had filled her lungs when she could no longer resist the urge to inhale.

Not dead, Little Fish—changed—together—together and between.

The unspoken words filled Trin's mind so forcefully that she winced at their intensity. 'What's happening?' *Who—how—confusion.*

She struggled to sit up. She felt the strong hands press into her back and help her. She wrenched her head sideways to see who was behind her. The face was pale, glistening. Trin scrambled across the sharp sand, trying to get away from the strange face, but the strong arms reached out and held her.

Trin panicked. *Stranger—bad.*

Safe—loved—calm—safe.

An overwhelming calmness washed over her. She let herself slump onto the gritty beach. *Confusion.* 'I don't understand,' she rasped.

A soft, faltering voice responded. 'I have a wonderful, unbelievable and perhaps unforgivable thing to share with you, Little Fish ... my darling daughter, Trin.'

'Daughter!'

Patience—trust. 'You will know the whole story soon enough.'

The wave of calm reinforced itself in Trin's mind.

'I am Rilla,' the shiny woman said slowly, as if she was out of practice with speaking. 'I am your mother.'

'Cut back.' Trin felt as though she was dropping into a noisy darkness.

Rilla held Trin firmly around the shoulders and hummed. The tune was one that Trin had always held in her heart. *My heart tells me that I love you ...*

Trin whispered the next phrase. '... more than all the little pearly shells.'

Then Rilla told her a story that matched the one her dad and Meg had told her ever since she was very young. A story about how her parents fell in love and were married, and of her birth, and happy times together in the rockpools, the gardens, and birthday parties. Then at that point in the story, when her mother died, Rilla's story branched away from the one Trin knew.

'I hid in the shallows, hoping the saltwater could stop me from being unwell, and it did help with some of it. There are caves beneath this place, so when I needed to be safe from eyes and storms, I went there. I could never have gone any further away. I stayed and watched my wonderful Marcus grieve. I felt the pain radiate from him and saw him lower the false me into a grave. He went up to the cliff-top gardens often, to be near my tree, and with me. I could feel that he was so full of sadness, and I sent him what love and comfort I could. I sent it to you too, Little Fish. I sent you our shell song to sooth you and make you feel loved.'

As Rilla said these words, Trin felt the echo of them inside her head and found herself believing what this impossible, shiny woman told her. Trin's stomach flipped and twisted, but the rest of her felt as if she was turning to stone. She felt so heavy with the weight of this new, fantastic reality.

'I couldn't leave this place, Trin. I need to spend much of my time in the sea or I become very ill. If I'd stayed with you I would have died. I had to make a most horrible choice, but I needed to watch over my wonderful daughter, even if I could only do it from afar.'

'I know how much Dad loved you, still loves you. He would have done anything.'

'He couldn't have helped.'

'I don't understand. Surely he could've done *something*. He has so much knowledge. He could have tried something.'

'It became more than the sickness.' Rilla had been kneeling, but now she wriggled, unfolding her legs and stretching them out in front of her.

Trin gasped.

Rilla's skin was slightly pearled. She wasn't wearing clothes, but she had a skirt of what looked like twined hair around her hips. Rilla's legs were long and tapered, ending in small, misshapen feet that extended out into frilled, transparent fins. Images of Kayn and Andy burst through Trin's mind. She could feel their finned tails wrapped around her legs, dragging her down.

Rilla held Trin's hands. *Nakki—gone—safe.*

A fresh calm trickled into Trin's mind. 'What, you're a ... mermaid, then?'

'Yes, you would say mermaid.' Rilla smiled. 'That's what the walker myths and fairytales called us.'

'Walkers?'

'People from the land, your father, you, the others.'

'And there are really mermaids?'

'We call ourselves the Abrax, the very first people.'

'So you're not human.' Trin's mind was squirming.

'I am ... human, I mean, we are the same. Our origin is the same. Though it's hard to imagine, once we were all one people, but long ago we found a way to change form, to allow the Abrax to move from the sea, to walk and live in the Above, which is what we call your world. Some of our people chose to ascend, and over the millennia the ancient truths about beings from the sea became part science, part missing-link theory, and part myth.'

'Until today.' Trin stared at her own skin, remembering when it had glowed. She touched her mother's hand. The skin looked anything but human. Trin stared at that skin, clenching her jaw, not wanting to hear the answer to her next question. 'If you are a mer—Abrax, what am I?'

'You are my daughter.'

'But how did any of that happen? Dad must have noticed. You look …' *Shiny.*

'Eons ago the Abrax created a liquid that caused our bodies to be transformed so we could live on land. I chose to use the catalyst and it changed me. When I met your father, I was almost a walker, although not as shiny, no fins, this cirrus was gone.' She brushed her hand across the hair skirt at her hips. 'But the effects of the catalyst were never guaranteed. The process mustn't have been complete because the changes started to unmake themselves. I became unwell—'

'You got sick, but I get sick, too!' Trin put her hands on her collarbones and touched her newly formed gill slits. She felt them ripple as air passed through them. 'I'm changing, too.' Her stomach squeezed and she swallowed down a mouthful of burning bile. 'What will I turn into?' Tears rolled down her face.

'The changes today were forced, Little Fish. The nakki gave you a potion, a serum.'

'The drink … Andy … the thing … gave me a drink. It tasted wrong.'

'In the ancient knowledge, there were other change agents apart from the catalyst. They must've used one of those.' Rilla squeezed Trin's hand. 'You wouldn't have changed if you hadn't taken the drink. You are who you are. We don't change without help.'

'I *did* change. Before Kayn and Andy arrived.' Trin glared at her impossible mother. 'The voices, signals, whatever this … *quimby* thing is that happens inside my head. I hear things.'

'I know.' Rilla smiled. 'I hear the echoes from the sea as well.' Then she laughed musically.

'What's so funny?'

'The signals you hear are called neumes. That's how we and other creatures communicate underwater, and some of them are messages that I've sent you. No matter what, I can't stop being your mother.' Rilla's cheeks were wet with tears.

'And the fish radar? That didn't always happen with me.'

'Skills like that grow in strength as younglings grow towards adulthood. Fish finding was one of my strongest skills, and it stayed strong even after I became a walker. I'm not surprised it's strong with you.'

'What a gene pool to swim in.' Trin found herself laughing at her unexpected joke. She felt air huffing through her new gills and her laughter stopped. 'I have gills!'

'Hush, Little Fish. Calm. If the gills are the only change you've experienced until now there won't be anything more. How do you feel?'

Trin took a deep breath and felt the ripple run through her new gills. 'I feel … okay.'

'You're a walker, Trin.' She pointed to Trin's feet and then to her own. She flexed her stunted fins and they flapped to and fro.

Trin copied the movement and gave a tiny laugh. 'No fins, crankin'. Sorry, no offence.'

'Don't worry.' Rilla wrapped her arm around Trin's shoulders.

'Worry? What about the other two, Kayne and Andy? They were like you were, before. They could walk, and they looked, well, everyone thought they looked normal, I mean human. Couldn't they just swim back here again?'

'They, we, the Abrax, can make ourselves appear as we want walkers to see us. It has to do with the way we communicate. We use the neume to send signals, and it has strong mental effects on walkers. That's what you've been experiencing in your mind. The Abrax stopped needing the neume after they left the sea, so that part of their brains grew weaker. Walkers can still easily receive neumes without ever recognising them as anything other than their own thoughts. We can place images and ideas into a walker's mind without them being aware of it. They have no way to stop it happening. That's how I hid my differences from your father and the others. It's also how the nakki, the ones you knew as Kayn and Andy, could appear normal to everyone at the station.'

'But we saw them walking.'

'All Abrax can walk if they need to—we have feet within our fins—but it would've meant pain beyond imagining for them. They were controlled by some very strong forces, so they would have had to simply tolerate the pain.'

'Won't they just come back and try again?'

'Believe me, they're gone forever. I neumed strongly and made them accept that they saw you and me dead, eaten by sharks.' Rilla thought it better not to share her neumes about Lana. 'Now that they've seen we are dead, the nakki serve no purpose so they will be planted in the hiisi-weed garden for what remains of their lives.'

'The what?'

'Later.' *Patience.*

'I don't understand why they wanted me. What did I do?'

'It wasn't you. It was because I chose to ascend. I saw that by working together, Abrax and walker, we could heal the damage to both worlds. I believe the Gathering of Colours, who are the leaders of the Abrax, would rather keep on hating the walkers than see a future where we could work together.'

'So the ... whoever, they just took me.' Trin tried to imagine what her fate might have been and shuddered. *Harm—death?*

Safe now. 'You and I are the link that could make the unification and healing happen, so some of the Abrax wanted to ensure that no one ever discovered we exist or others might choose to ascend also.' Rilla flashed an image of the grizzly illusion of the shark attack.

'So you're a shubee, you faked it all.'

'Now that we're believed to be dead there's no longer a threat.' Rilla smiled.

Trin tried to take in the idea of where she might have ended up. *Wonder—curiosity.* She overflowed with questions about the world her mother had grown up in.

'I know, there's much to understand and accept. I'll show you.' Rilla encircled Trin in her arms.

Amazing images filled Trin's head: people swimming, no, they were Abrax. Pearled, sleek, glimmering bodies streaming through dark blue water with their tails flashing. The incredible creatures glowed all the colours of the rainbow. Images and words flashed into Trin's awareness. *Lemuria—home.* Trin saw a sunken valley inside a huge underwater cavern. Within the cavern was a city that looked as though it had grown from the coral floor of the cave.

Family. Glimmering faces flashed through her awareness, along with regret and longing. Then, with a great burst of love and pride, images unspooled of Trin and her father and their lives at the station, as seen through her mother's eyes.

Trin hugged her mother. Pressing her face hard into Rilla's neck, she felt the feathery edge of gills flutter against her cheek.

Eons of history and a wealth of new knowledge about the sea and her ancestral home were gushing into Trin's mind, spilling over the edges. She thought the neume, as her unexpected mother called it, was an amazingly effective way of communicating, fast and thorough. Along with this flood of information came the comforting realisation that the mysterious thoughts and feelings Trin had been experiencing had a source.

She wasn't sick or insane; she was Abrax.

And now her mother was using these neumes to calm her, and help her understand and accept this impossible discovery.

THE ABOVE

The jagged folds in the rock dug into Mal and Sharly's bare feet as they ran back along the ledge towards the station. As soon as they rounded the headland, they started shouting to raise the alarm. People rushed out of caves and down snakes as an automatic response honed by the frequent safety drills.

'Trin's missing,' yelled Mal. 'So are Andy and Kayn. Something grabbed us from under the water, but we managed to get free.'

'Where were they last?' Meg asked Mal, swinging a rescue kit over her shoulder.

She placed a firm and steadying hand on Marcus's arm. 'I know you want to go, but you're not on the rescue detail today, okay?' She nodded to Jasper, who moved in close and gripped Marcus firmly to support him as he crumpled to the ground.

'Where?' she asked, turning back to Mal.

'Out around the headland.'

Mal and Sharly turned and ran, leading Meg back along the shelf.

'Trin went ahead with Andy,' Mal said as they ran, 'and then we lost sight of Kayn, and somehow we got snagged.' Mal didn't even try to describe the strange weedy creatures. 'Maybe Kayn was caught, too, and Trin and Andy.'

'Doubtful,' mumbled Sharly. She thought it more likely that Kayn had created the strange weed monsters rather than been a victim of them. She remembered those blurred, shimmering blue visions she had teased Trin about. 'I should never have let her go alone with Andy.' Sharly said, swallowing a sob.

THE BETWEEN

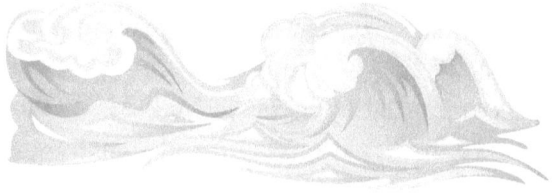

They're coming,' said Rilla, 'Sharly, Mal, Meg, some of the others. They'll search here soon. This isn't the time for a reunion, no matter how much I yearn to be with Marcus, or how hard it is to let go of your hand.'

Trin knew as well as her mother that this new truth, and the 'Between' world that her mother had described, and that she had become a part of today, needed to remain a secret. 'It'll be so hard to just return home like none of this has happened.'

'For now, that's what you have to do.' Rilla's eyes glazed over and she stared out into a great distant awareness. 'There's a storm coming and it'll be a big one.'

'You can't stay here.'

'I'll be fine, as I always am.'

Trin squeezed her mother's hands. As she did, she felt neumes coming from Sharly and Mal. And a blast of panicked concern from her father. She hugged her mother tightly. The idea of letting go again felt like the hardest thing she would ever do.

Her mother moved away and ran a gentle hand over one of Trin's new gills. Her face was filled with warm pride. 'Put on the shirt. You should try to keep this wonderful new thing a secret.' She handed Trin a raggedy old station shirt to cover her new gills.

'It *is* a wonderful thing,' said Trin breathlessly, pulling on the shirt and fumbling with a few of the buttons.

The agitated sea was starting to slam into the island, splashing up high into the air and making dark spots on the bare rock as Trin ran for the channel. *Milkshake in a blender.* She looked at the channel, which was now frothing and wild, and dived in.

Growling. There was an angry sound all around her, like a rasping breath as the water forced itself backwards and forwards through the narrow passage of the Blender. It pushed and twisted her, and made her think a pair of giant blue hands, one second pushing her down and the next trying to smash her up onto the rocks. She fought to come up for air and was pushed down by a wave.

She fought and scrambled, clawing to get to the churning surface to steal a precious breath.

Gulp—breathe—gulp.

She remembered her gills and tried to fight her body's lifelong instinct to breathe air.

Calm—the current will lead you to the edge— then lift.

Trin's mind filled with images of disking. She knew her mother had watched the disking and was giving her tips to overcome the wedge in the channel.

Gulp. Trin's body finally accepted her new anatomy and let her gills work for her. Now she could concentrate on feeling the currents. She listened to the water, reached out to sense its rhythms. She was getting a feel for the lift in the Blender, but there were still rocks that she didn't want to wipe out on when she got to the other side of the channel.

THE ABOVE

Sharly had run hard, fuelled by her feelings of guilt for letting Trin go off on her own. 'I see her,' she screamed over her shoulder as she dived into the water. Trin had surfaced for a moment and then disappeared again.

Sharly duck-dived to search for Trin. A twisting current grabbed hold of Sharly and pushed her down. Then she felt a hand. She grabbed desperately for Trin's arm and started kicking with all her strength to pull her to the surface. The twisting current wrenched them both sideways. Sharly clung to Trin as they were swept against the rocks. Trin was pushing her away.

Sharly fought to help her, but she was running out of air. Her mind was becoming a storm of sparks as her brain became starved of oxygen. Finally, Trin pushed, and Sharly went with her.

They broke the surface of the water and Sharly realised she had lost her sense of where the surface was, and she had been pushing them downwards. Trin had pushed upwards and saved them both. Sharly gasped and choked, trying to breathe as the waves smashed into her face.

'We're going to disk in,' Trin screamed in her ear. 'Feel for the lift, okay?'

'Crank,' choked Sharly.

The next wave smacked them both back under the water. It felt as though their legs were being twisted in the opposite direction to their bodies. Then they were lifted up, and down again, and forward. Trin squeezed Sharly's wrist.

The next upwards surge was big. Trin tugged them down deeper in the water for a moment and twisted them around, and now the wave was forcing itself into Sharly's face. She made desperate frightened noises with the last breath she had. Trin wrapped her arms around her and then … woof. They were lifted and pushed into the air, surrounded by a blizzard of seaspray. Then they were falling. There was no net this time. They landed hard, on their backs on the rock ledge.

A tangle of arms grabbed them and pulled them away from the edge before the next surge could dump down on them and sweep them back into the channel again.

Trin fumbled to check that the shirt was still buttoned up, and squinted the saltwater out of her eyes. She saw her father, then Mal, Meg, Jasper. Her dad was crying. He folded himself up next to her on the rocks and wrapped her in a vice-like hug. She could feel the sobs heaving in his chest.

Calm—safe—love, she neumed. Her father relaxed slightly. 'I'm all right, Dad, really.' She hugged him. She borrowed the neume of being tangled in the hostile weed from Sharly's mind and didn't wait to be asked. 'I was caught in some weed. By the time I could get free I'd drifted into the Blender. I don't know what happened to Andy,' she added. 'Is he all right?'

'We don't know about Kayn and Andy yet,' said Meg.

Trin reached for Sharly's hand. 'Thanks, Sharls, if it wasn't for you …'

Meg moved from checking on Sharly and came over to examine Trin.

Gills! 'I'm fine, Meg, really.' She pretended to shiver and pulled the old shirt up close around her neck, securing the very top button.

'I really need to have a good look at you,' said Meg.

Trin took a tighter grip on the soggy shirt, pretending to shiver. She knew all she could do was delay sharing her new truth. 'I'm crankin', Meg, just cold. Could we do this back at the sickbay?' She shivered, snuggling deeper into her father's arms.

The storm siren started screaming.

'We better go,' said Mal.

'Can you run?' Meg asked Trin.

'Just watch me.' Trin hugged her father once more, then stood and took off running.

A knife of lightning speared the sea, causing the blackening sky to flare. All six of them were running. The wind screeched, lashing the sea up into mountains. As they ran, waves slammed into the rock ledge and spewed up into the sky. Then they fell back down, dumping on the runners and threatening to wash them off the rocks.

By the time they had reached the shelter of the station, the rain was blowing against the cliffs in blinding diagonal sheets. Everyone ran straight for the control centre on the lowest level. Trin took advantage of the confusion caused by the blinding rain and changed course, heading for the ladder. She was going to climb for her cave. That would give her some time to figure out how to hide her gills, or how to share her fantastic secret, and decide whom to tell first. She hoped desperately that Sharly would notice what she'd done and follow her.

As she reached the top of the first ladder, Trin saw that the sea was withdrawing from the rocky corridor of the Funnel. When the water pulled away like that, it meant the surge would be big. She glanced out to sea and saw a howling grey cliff of water. No turning back for the lower levels now that she had passed the halfway point from the safety of the control centre.

As she took the turn and started on the second ladder, she saw Sharly three steps behind her, and in the blurry distance she saw Meg and Jasper holding her father as they stared out the door of the control centre. They were looking from her to the approaching wall of water.

Sharly was screaming something at her, but the roar was drowning out everything. The ladder shook in the wind, threatening to come loose from the wall. The bolts that secured it to the rocks groaned and rattled in their anchor holes. Trin and Sharly climbed hard. The ladder rattled again violently and Sharly slipped. Trin stopped, turned and hooked an exhausted noodle arm around Sharly and hoisted her back to her feet, and then they took off again.

The building-sized wave was cresting. *Please*, begged Trin, *let us get to the cave before the wave does*. Keeping this secret wasn't worth risking her best friend's life.

Trin jumped from the second-last step of the ladder and rolled into the cave. As she righted herself, she flicked the release latch on the storm door. It hissed out of its cradle, ready to close when she hit the engage switch. Sharly's hand came over the ledge and Trin pulled her all the way in. She touched Sharly's bracelet to the scanner and then her own. The monitor in the control centre would show Dad and Meg that they were up here and safe.

The wave filled the whole sky now.

Trin slammed the button to engage the storm seal. The mechanism fought against the force of the wind and slowly moved itself into place ... too slowly.

Trin and Sharly scuttled back into the cave, grabbing for their harnesses. They'd been taught in storm drills about the need to harness up and clip onto the anchor points on the rear wall. This was the first time they had even come close to needing it. The storm door had always been enough, but it wasn't closed yet. They fumbled into their harness, clipped on and waited. The storm door finally hissed shut and sealed.

THE BETWEEN

Ihe storm had lasted for hours. Once Trin and Sharly had stopped clinging to each other, they de-harnessed and ate a dinner of emergency rations by torchlight. Trin used the hours to tell Sharly what had happened. Sharly only asked about seven million questions and looked at Trin's gills three thousand times before she believed her. Trin knew Sharly would keep her secret, but she would have to tell the others soon.

Sharly was snoring quietly as Trin cracked the storm seal and sat herself on the cave ledge to watch the sun rise over the languid water. No one else was moving around down on the shelf, which was blanketed with huge mounds of kelp.

A rippling neume flowed into Trin's awareness and she looked out towards the island. She could see Rilla— her mum—silhouetted against the first glow of the day. She waved and then the tiny silhouette was gone again.

Trin smiled. *Good morning—safe?*

Very good morning—safe.

Trin thought of her mother trapped between two worlds, never able to be truly a part of either place. She could only exist there, in the place between the ocean and the land.

Trin ran her hands across her fluttering gills. She was part of that place now, too. Soon she would need to tell Meg her secret, show her the amazing changes, and then collude with her to find the best way to tell her dad about the real-life myth he had been a part of for all these years.

Trin's face burned. What if he couldn't forgive her mother for deceiving him? But maybe he always felt she was there, and that's why he'd never stopped pining for her. Things would be fine. Trin would use neumes so her dad would realise the wonderful truth gently. Then all three of them would swim in the rock pools together like they used to.

The world of the Above was definitely not yet ready for the Abrax, Trin knew that, so she would need to be the gatekeeper and the conduit between the two worlds.

The healing work could continue. Having two scientists at the station that could fish-talk and spend hours researching under water would be a great benefit for continuing the healing work.

Acknowledgements

Thank you to Julieann Wallace for casting your editing eagle eye over my sub-marine ramblings.

Thank you to Christine Titheradge for the great story development chatter and for being my mermaid expert.

To Michelle Worthington and all the supportive and creative souls in Share Your Story Australia, thanks for all the practical advice and sparkling inspiration.

Thank you to Anthony Puttee, Penny Springthorpe and the team at Book Cover Cafe for your creative insights and professional support.

Other titles from Martii Maclean

If I Die Before I Wake

Not all tales have the ever after you might expect. Vreni is fifteen and cursed. She has slept and woken at the whim of the curse since her birth over a century ago. She is kept isolated from the world by her family, and yearns for a normal life. Her family's guardians ask her to learn the secrets of their magic and help them retrieve what remains of the sleeping potion from the evil alchemists who created it. With these last few drops, they hope to create a cure and set Vreni and her family free from the curse.

Weird Weirder Weirdest

In this collection of quirky tales, peculiar short stories will take you to weird worlds just beyond the here and now: strange places where kids can control time, where playing is against the law, and where ragdolls can become real girls. In these places magic can be found everywhere, even in cakes and pens and running shoes. Come and take a look. It's not too far … just beyond the here and now.

About the Author

Martii Maclean lives in a tin shack by the sea catching seagulls, which she uses to make delicious pies, and writing weird stories. She likes going for long bicycle rides with her cat, who always wears aviator goggles to stop her whiskers blowing up into her eyes as they speed down to the beach to search for mermaid eggs.

Visit **martiimaclean.com** to find out more about Martii, get your free short story, and find out about free resources and upcoming events.